The Upper Hand

WITHDRAWN

Also by Stuart Hood

NOVELS

The Circle of the Minotaur
Since the Fall
A Storm from Paradise

NON-FICTION

Carlino
On Television
The Mass Media

TRANSLATIONS

Riccardo Bacchelli, *The Mill on the Po*
Dino Buzzati, *The Tartar Steppe*
The Diaries of Ciano
Ennio Flaiano, *Mariam*
Erich Fried, *100 Poems without a Country*
Ernst Jünger, *On the Marble Cliffs*
Ernst Jünger, *African Diversions*
Dacia Maraini, *The Holiday*
Pier Paolo Pasolini, *Lutheran Letters*
Theodor Plivier, *Moscow*

The Upper Hand

STUART HOOD

CARCANET

First published in Great Britain 1987 by
Carcanet Press Limited
208–212 Corn Exchange Buildings
Manchester M4 3BQ

Carcanet
198 Sixth Avenue
New York, New York 10013

British Library Cataloguing in Publication Data
Hood, Stuart
The upper hand.
I. Title
823′.914 [F]   PR6058.054/

ISBN 0-85635-719-7

The publisher acknowledges financial assistance
from the Arts Council of Great Britain

Typeset in 11/13pt Bembo by Paragon Photoset, Aylesbury
Printed in England by SRP Ltd, Exeter

para la osita blanca que vaga
por las selvas de mi corazón

PART I

On the north-east coast of Scotland in the last days of September there can be a sequence of halcyon days. The sea is warm, milky and smooth with an almost imperceptible swell like the rise and fall of a sleeper's breast, sending little waves lapping gently on to the sand. The children are back at school. The summer visitors are gone, although the tall poles that mark the safe bathing area are still there, almost totally submerged at high tide, as are the poles of the salmon nets, which run a hundred yards or so out to sea to form a false river bank along which the glinting fish come nosing in and are caught in the arrow-shaped nets. The spear-grass of the dunes is browning. Little sea-birds bob and scurry round the skirts of the waves. Beyond the nets the terns hover and dive, throwing up plumes of water.

That we should be sitting there on a fine September afternoon, talking, laughing, drying off after a long swim beyond the farthest pole of the salmon nets, meant that we had done with school and were idling through the end of summer until the time came for us to scatter to college or university. We had grown up together. Had played together. Together had fidgetted through long winter afternoons, knowing that at the other end of the town from the school the skating pond was frozen and bearing. Had the same stories about our teachers, the same knack of taking off their tics and mannerisms. We belonged firmly to the lower to middle reaches of town society. My father was a minister of a sparsely attended Free Church. The others were the sons respectively of the harbourmaster,

7

of a primary schoolteacher, of a widow who was a maid in a hotel, and of the owner of an ice-cream parlour. He had the dark skin of his Neapolitan parents but spoke with the marked local accent we all shared. There was in us a sense of excitement tinged with a certain nervousness. We masked it with bravado, proclaiming that the only motto for the future was: 'Try anything once.' We were all virgins, sex being one of the things we had not so far tried. Opportunity had not offered itself and the scrutiny of a small-town community did not encourage adventures. It was true that there had been boys in our class who had boasted of sexual experience — mostly in the back row of the local flea-pit where there were double seats for couples, or among the high grass of the dunes; but significantly they had all left — had had to leave rather — in their third or, at latest, fourth year of secondary school to get a job. What marked us off was that our parents had contrived to let us stay on, enjoying certain licensed liberties in our last year in the sixth form, such as the right to take periods off to study on our own and in general to have the run of the school. This meant, among other things, the opportunity — for the boys at least — to go up on some vague excuse into the school's gilt classical dome where a plaster copy of the Venus de Milo was chastely stowed away. She was strangely small. There was a peculiar excitement in the moment when, for a dare, I placed my hand on her breast and ran it over the stomach. Although we were used to bathing with girls from our class — dressing and undressing at a modest distance from each other in the dunes — none of us had seen a fully naked woman and could only speculate about the statue's anatomical accuracy; but we shared a suspicion that it was somehow defective.

On this September afternoon, however, we were discussing something other than sex. Someone had defiantly announced that there was no difference in value between an Edgar Wallace thriller and any of the set books we had had to read at school: *The Mill on the Floss, The Heart of Midlothian, A Tale of Two Cities.* I was at a disadvantage, for thrillers and such like 'trash'

8

were strictly forbidden at home and the reading of a French novel like *Madame Bovary*, which I had discovered in a cupboard in the French classroom — complete with the arguments and quotations used by the prosecution at its trial for indecency — was sanctioned only out of ignorance and the feeling that though French and therefore by definition morally suspect, it was the kind of thing that stood one in good stead in the Edinburgh University Bursary Competition in which, alas, I proved a disappointment by coming out only twentieth. But I was strong in my defence on the grounds that there was a seriousness about certain works that raised them far above Edgar Wallace and any other rubbish you could get on railway bookstalls. A good book, I reminded my listeners sententiously, is the precious life-blood of a master spirit. But the others had been distracted by the noise of a motorcycle coming to a stop on the road just above our heads. The discussion died.

A couple of minutes later a boy of our own age appeared over the crest of the dunes and slithered down towards us. He was wearing a faded blazer with purple stripes. The collar of his tennis shirt stood up in a negligent but somehow elegant ruff round his neck. His face was brown; the cheeks slightly ruddy; but it was his hair that struck me. It was dark and soft and fell over his brow in a gentle silky mass.

When he reached the bottom of the dune we received him in suspicious silence. We knew perfectly well who he was: Colin Elphinstone of Usan, where his parents lived in a slightly neglected house at the end of a long drive with a deserted gate-house and a pillared entrance, on which were the half-defaced quarterings of his family and their motto: *Tenaciter*. In short, a different species from ourselves. Sometimes when we were younger and felt adventurous, we would dash through the entrance on our bicycles and down the drive to the front of the house, which looked across a wide bay. At the far end, beyond tempting but treacherous sands, a ruined red-sandstone keep stood like a decayed molar. Then we would ride in circles on the gravel until someone — a maid or one of Colin's unexpectedly old parents — would appear at the high drawing-room windows and rap on the pane to tell us to clear off. We made one last defiant round on the gravel and then rode away, plucking a twig from a flowering shrub as a trophy, laughing and capering in our saddles. Colin we usually saw only in summer. Even as a young boy he played for the local cricket team along with the sons of the big farmers from round about and of the men who ran the town: the owner of the salmon fisheries along the coast, the bank manager, the rector of the High School, which we all attended but whose son was at some minor Scottish public school. Sitting on our bicycles we looked over the fence of the sports ground to watch Colin walk out to the crease with a typical blend of confidence and grace to face the bowling. Next day the local paper would talk about the fine innings of Master Colin Elphinstone, praise the stylishness of his batting and the accuracy of his fielding. We did not play cricket, which we despised as a slow, boring game reserved for the gentry. We had no place in the pavilion among the young men in white flannels and the young women in summer dresses who watched, clapped, displayed themselves and applauded Colin as he walked back from the pitch and lifted his purple and white cap in acknowledgement. But the golf links were ours — town land on which we played by right. We knew the course by heart; knew how to play off into the wind along the crest of the dunes and the right club to use if your ball was blown into the spear-grass and the drifted sand. It was our native heath and we felt invincible on it. So it was with some surprise that we heard him say:

'Hello, I was thinking of getting up a golf match' — he pronounced it in a funny way: 'goff' — 'and wondered if you chaps would feel like putting up a team.'

We considered the suggestion in silence.

'Who against?' someone asked.

'Oh, a scratch lot. Some chaps from my school up here for the hols.'

There was another silence.

'Aye, we'll tak ye on at gowff.'

The deliberate use of dialect was an index of our sense of distance and difference.

He said 'Right', proposed the following Saturday and left with a 'Cheerio.' We listened to him starting up his motorcycle, heard him turn up the throttle and drive off with a quick change of gears. As the noise died away we burst out laughing and rolled in the sand, imitating his accent. Then there was a discussion that ranged over his dress, his general appearance and the probability of beating his side. I took little part for I was puzzling over my sense of having been confronted by someone of my own sex who was — the word was inescapable — beautiful. Asked for my opinion I covered my confusion by hamming — in the Highland accent of our English teacher — Chaucer's description of the young squire on that pilgrimage to Canterbury: 'He was as fresh as is the month of May.' In their laughter they did not notice that I had blushed.

I was drawn against him as I had both hoped and feared. He had a good eye and a natural swing but kept forcing it, so that he either sliced or hooked and wandered erratically from one side of the fairway to the other. I realized with a mixture of excitement and sadness that if I could play a reasonably steady game I was more or less bound to beat him. By the turn I was three up. Then the course left the dunes with their treacherous patches of wind-blown sand and tricky reverse slopes; on the level he did better and made me fight to retain my lead. At the fourteenth he sliced badly. The ball hovered in the wind and fell in a graceful parabola into a clump of whin bushes. 'Bad luck,' I said. 'For Christ's sake, will you stop saying bad luck when it's simply bad play,' he retorted. When we came to the last hole I was three up again. A long straight drive with the wind off the sea behind it, a shot with a number one iron that left a tiny clean patch of bare earth where the head of the club had lifted the ball to land it on the green and a couple of putts clinched, as the local paper said, my victory. He shook my hand and his congratulations sounded genuine; so I said some-

11

thing about practically living on the links. 'Maybe we'll have a return match one day,' he said as he revved up his motorcycle and drove off.

There was no return match although he was back at Usan next summer. We had all got jobs in our university vacation on the fruit farm which stretched its long drills of raspberry bushes above the fishing village of Usan; at the height of the season we worked on Saturdays too, so a match would in any case have been difficult to arrange. Besides, Colin apparently had other interests. Gossip said they were centred on Janet Munro, the daughter of the minister of a country parish a couple of miles inland. But we told ourselves he was scared of being licked again. Meantime we sat all day in the fields on our high stools in front of our weighing-scales: tally-clerks who recorded each picker's poundage and earnings. Behind me was the horse-drawn float on which the punnets mounted. The aroma of the warm fruit was heady but, after the first day when I had eaten my fill, I had no appetite for it. The horse stood patiently, whisked its tail, farted from time to time and pawed the dry earth at the end of the rig. Among the high bushes the heads of the girls and women bobbed as they picked with a steady circling movement that led them from bush to bush: seals in a sea of green. As their baskets filled they brought them to the end of the drill and then on to the scales for me to weigh. In part they were landward people from the cottar-houses round the church where Janet Munro's widower father preached but the bulk were fisher-folk from Usan, where the old women sat in the doorways baiting with mussels the mile-long lines for the men who sailed at dawn and brought back at midday haddock, cod, halibut, sole, for sale at the dockside. Normally these same girls worked in the jute-mill. Its mournful hooter called them across by ferry on a couple of days a week to the ruined wharves and rusty sidings where only two boats regularly moored: the beer boat and the potato boat, which between them supplied the pubs and fish-

and-chip shops of Tyneside. But now the mill was closed for holidays that — given the Depression — might extend long enough. These Usan girls were bold, with none of the reserve of the girls in our class at school — now like ourselves under-graduates or training to be teachers of gym or domestic science. It is true that one had been hastily married — somewhat beneath her, for her father was a dentist — to the randy son of a publican. Her fall, according to the aunt who looked after my sister and myself, was entirely due to goings-on in a beach-hut. If she had anything to do with it, she announced over breakfast on the morning of the wedding, she would have the huts removed. In any case they were right eye-sores. So we knew that the proximity of male and female could have troub-ling consequences; but none of us was prepared for the sexual frankness of the fisher-lassies, who offered unspecified favours if one were to add a pound or two to their day's weight tally. As they did so they peered over my shoulder to check the figures in my book, deliberately pressing their breasts against my back. Then they would draw back with a laugh, drop a berry down my shirt and squash it with a slap. From among the bushes their friends watched and laughed. But we tally-clerks were, as a group, too sensible of the need to preserve reputations — our own and our parents' — and too ignorantly afraid to accept the invitation to 'come up a drill' or to take a walk in the dunes that evening. The girls had their revenge on us for our apparent indifference. Thus as I walked through the town with my aunt — something I was generally at pains to avoid — they would greet me ostentatiously so that my aunt would ask in her precise Edinburgh accent: 'And who are these lassies, I would like to know, waving to you, John Melville. They don't look like High School girls to me. Very common.' I would mumble something about 'girls from the berries' and we would pass on.

It was an oppressive day in August of that summer. The tidal basin behind the town was a mottled mirror on which clouds and an occasional cat's-paw of wind drew shifting patterns. My carter was plaiting a straw into a favour for his button-hole, to wear on Saturday night when he would take his girl over the dunes for what he called 'a mow'. He raised his head at the sound of a motorcycle coming down the hill behind us. It was Colin Elphinstone, masked with goggles, bent over the handlebars, with his shirt ballooning in the wind. 'Aye,' remarked the carter, 'he'll have been up at the manse. She'll have been going over his Catechism with him, I expect.' He laughed and spat and was silent. Half-an-hour later there was the clip-clop of hooves and a pony and trap came sedately down the road. The girl who held the reins wore a white blouse with a sailor collar and a wide straw hat. It was Janet Munro. I had known her as a child, for our fathers, both being of the cloth and both widowers, would call on each other to discuss church matters and the problem of bringing up bairns without a mother. As they talked the two of us would amuse ourselves quietly at the other end of the room or else escape to the hay-shed at the side of the manse where we invented a game called 'bears'. It involved crawling about in the hay and growling at each other. Then one of us would raise a paw and we would fight in a way that was half savage, half gentle. In one of these tussles her skirt rode up and I saw to my amazement, above her stocking, white — and as it seemed to me — incredibly soft and silky flesh. She tugged her skirt down angrily and said: 'I'll tell your father — no, I'll tell your auntie you looked.' I begged her not to and after a while she said perhaps she'd let me off this time. So she spared me but we played no more 'bears'. Then for some years she disappeared into a ladies' college in Edinburgh and on her rare visits to town was very distant, barely recognizing me in the street. After all she was, as my aunt pointed out, a little heiress and very well connected on her late mother's side. Now as she drove past us to the slow pace of the pony I looked hard at her over the hedge at the end of the field. There was no spark of recognition. She clicked her tongue and the pony momentarily broke into a reluctant trot. 'Aye,' said the carter, 'white for chastity.' Then he told me how people swore young Elphinstone had been seen climbing up a ladder to her bedroom where he had stayed all night. Back in the hut at the farmyard where we checked our tallies, played pontoon for trivial stakes and argued about morals and politics, I told the story of the ladder. We laughed a lot, not without envy.

Colin Elphinstone turned up at Edinburgh University in 1936, in my second year, for reasons that were obscure. One rumour was that he had been sent down from Oxford for playing a record of the *Internationale* very loudly from a punt at dawn on May Day just as madrigal singers were about to strike up from the top of Magdalen College tower. The authorities were not pleased, people said, especially since the BBC had sent down a recording-van for the occasion. Another version was that he had fallen in love with an actress whom he met when he was carrying a spear in an OUDS production of *Troilus and Cressida*. Her husband had threatened divorce proceedings and Colin had had to go into exile in the North until things blew over. At all events there he suddenly was in the Old Quad, helping to set up a film camera with some students from the Art History Department, who were notoriously upper-class, bohemian and cliquey. I felt a start of pleasure at the sight of him but made no approach that day. He did not see me for he was playing some role in the film which involved walking along the parapet of the Quad, tossing his scarf over his shoulder, running his hand through his hair to lift it from his brow, and pretending to stumble and fall, except that he recovered himself with a dancer's grace, jumped lightly down and ran out into the street. It was entirely to be expected that he should join this select band of aesthetes who attended seminars somewhere in the dome high above the Quad, where their teacher was a bohemian who had run off with someone else's wife, instead of taking his place with the rest of us in the high-tiered lecture-rooms. There a couple of hundred boys and girls sat quietly taking notes of lectures that were repeated verbatim year after year and did little more than précis standard text-books. Occasionally we would be moved to impatience

15

or disapproval by a lecturer who spoke too quickly or overran the allotted time. Then we would stamp on the floor and send a thunder-roll echoing out into the Quad.

We met at last at the Dialectic Society where Colin opened a debate on the motion That man owes more to Marx than to Moses. As he spoke he leaned over the lectern with a languid grace that led my neighbour to inquire in a loud whisper whether he was a pansy; which I firmly denied. At the beginning of his speech Colin got a couple of quick laughs by apologizing for his Sassenach accent and then reminding us that his family motto was 'Tenaciter', which could be translated into guid braid Scots as: 'Haud fast.' He drew our attention, too, to the fact that, if one of his ancestors had signed the Solemn League and Covenant of 1643 in order to preserve the reformed religion in Scotland, another had been 'out' in the Forty-Five; which showed that politically his folk had always been willing to follow their consciences — and that was what he proposed to do this evening. He was, he hastened to say, greatly honoured to have been invited, although a newcomer and a 'fresher', to speak in this room and as a member of a society which had numbered among its members Robert Louis Stevenson and, further back, men who had written for the *Edinburgh Review* — not to mention the advocates, philosophers and economists, whose names were emblazoned on the roll of presidents of this ancient and learned society.

He went on to argue, as reported in the next issue of *The Student*, that it had been Marx's great and indeed unique achievement to provide us, through the labour theory of value, with a key which made possible a clear understanding of the mechanics of capitalist production. Capitalism, he maintained, would in its purest, theoretical form work thus: A worker would be paid no more for his labour than sufficed to recharge his energies so as to enable him to continue to work and to reproduce himself in a new generation of workers. It was the aim of the good — that is to say, the efficient — capitalist to keep the wages of the worker as close to the subsistence level as possible. But it took only a small portion of the worker's day to produce the value paid by the capitalist for his labour-power. The two, three, four or more hours of labour that went to complete the working day produced surplus value. It was from this surplus value that the capitalist derived his profits. If this terrible equation had been, as some supporters of capitalism might argue, distorted, then it was because the workers of all lands, the whole world of organized labour, had forced concessions out of the hard-faced men who operated the system. (Here, *The Student* noted, there was hissing and cheers.) But these concessions, wrung from unwilling industrialists, did not go far enough. A truly just society would distribute the wealth workers create to those same workers by socializing the means of production and ending private ownership in any shape or form. But such a truly just society could only be the result of the overthrow of the present system and its replacement by another. In Marxism we had to hand an instrument called dialectical materialism, which must surely appeal to his audience as members of the Dialectic Society, an instrument with which to set in motion the mechanisms of social change on a scientific basis as was already happening in a great country — dare he? need he name it? — in the East. He called on his audience to agree that freedom was the recognition of necessity — the recognition that it was necessary to change the world and not merely to explain it, that Marxism was an immense, unrivalled contribution to mankind's store of knowledge. He therefore proposed to the members of the learned society the motion that man undoubtedly owes more to Marx than to Moses in the certainty that they would vote overwhelmingly for it, and not allow themselves to be bamboozled by religious mysticism, however brilliantly it might be presented — as he had no doubt it would be — and whatever specious arguments were deployed in its defence.

He sat down to loud applause from his friends at the back of the hall, who had to be called to order by the chair before he could invite the opponent of the motion to speak. He was a law student who, I presumed, must be Jewish. Judaism was still a mystery to me. Jews inhabited the Old Testament, where their actions and moral code demonstrated (according to my aunt) that they were the forerunners of Scottish Presbyterianism and more particularly of that variety to which she herself belonged: the United Free Kirk. In the New Testament they were more problematic, for did they not demand of Pontius Pilate that he hand over Jesus that he might be put to death? But this, my aunt explained, was the work of the Pharisees whom she equated with the papacy, Episcopalianism and the Established Church of Scotland. So it was with some curiosity that I listened to the speaker, who was quick, animated and witty but given to extravagant tropes and convoluted jokes. Thus he kept addressing the chair as 'M'Lud' and then apologized elaborately for forgetting where he was and that he was not pleading for some criminal at the bar but arguing a case in front of the intelligent and learned members of a famous society — but still, in a certain sense, pleading for one of the greatest and wisest men who had ever trodden this earth. Moses, he wished to remind us, had us forever in his debt if only for one thing — the idea of the Sabbath, the concept that human beings deserve, nay require absolutely to have one day set aside by the Law for rest from their labours. Some sceptics might urge that the Sabbath was not the invention of Moses, for had not the Creator himself at the beginning of the world rested on the seventh day from all the work he had made and sanctified it. But the Sabbath stood at the heart of the Mosaic code. It was of minor importance to the speaker that for himself the Sabbath began when the first star appeared in the evening sky on Friday and extended all through Saturday — Shabbat — whereas his audience no doubt kept Sunday holy as their Sabbath. Was it not interesting, he added, that precisely in Scotland the same word was habitually used for the day of rest as in his own infinitely older religion? But that was by the way, what he wished to stress was that the Sabbath was among the great social advances of all time — one which, in its awe-inspiring simplicity and logicality, far outdid the Hegelian mumbo-jumbo perpetrated by Marx, who like Job had been visited with boils but had not learned humility from the experience, and by his well-named guardian, Engels, that fox-hunting womaniser who had himself extracted surplus value from workers in Manchester. He adjured us to disregard talk of labour theories of value and dialectical materialism. He believed fervently in the dialectic, which was a process of reasoning as old as Socrates. In the name of that same dialectic he begged us to vote for true social progress and to disregard those who although they spoke — if he might be allowed to misquote another famous Jew — with the tongues of Marx and of Engels yet lacked the greatest of all virtues: charity. He calmly, nay confidently, expected our unanimous support.

In the event, after a ragged debate in which some of Colin's friends made points about the backwardness of Judaism's dietary laws and the colonialist attitude of the Zionist settlers in Palestine towards the Arab population, he was narrowly defeated. I cast my vote for the motion chiefly as an expression of my anti-Sabbatariansim — a retrospective protest against all those long Sunday afternoons with half-drawn blinds when all play, all reading (except improving books) was forbidden and the summer hours were wasted. After the vote I went up to where Colin was receiving the congratulations of his friends. His face was still flushed; his lips very red; his eyes bright and slightly dilated. As they spoke and laughed he kept raising one hand to brush the soft hair away from his forehead on which one could see tiny beads of sweat. I managed to squeeze in close enough to catch his attention. 'Oh, hello,' he said after a moment's hesitation as he tried to place me, 'I hope you voted for Marx and me. You must come round to my digs and have a talk sometime. I've got a sort of discussion group going, if you're interested.' I said I'd like to very much. It was his apparent warmth and directness that caught me; yet as I walked home to my digs I wondered whether it was more than good manners, wondered, if fact, if he really knew who I was. I was by no means sure but hoped my doubts might be proved wrong.

19

It was not long after the debate that I finally determined to visit Mr Halcro. My aunt had been insistent that I should look him up as someone who could put in a good word for me when I graduated and it came to getting a job; but her insistence only made me stubbornly reluctant. I had learnt meanwhile that he was a powerful figure in the University, although not a member of it, as administrator of a bursary fund set up by successful graduates from my part of the world who proclaimed at annual dinners the importance of bettering oneself and talked about lads progressing from the tail of the plough to high office or solid wealth — although I doubted that many of them came from quite such humble origins. Mr Halcro, according to my aunt, had known my mother when she was a student-teacher in some tough working-class school down the Royal Mile. There could be no harm, as she put it, in seeing what 'auld acquaintance' could do for me. In my first year I cavilled at the idea. In the spring term of my second year I was beginning to find that my exiguous bursary — one available only to sons and daughters of the manse — left me little after I had paid my fees, bought text-books and paid my landlady for digs on the other side of Bruntsfield Links. Perhaps Mr Halcro might consider me a suitable case for a subvention. So I found his office which was in Hanover Street at the top of a long flight of stone stairs. His receptionist, a chilly lady with a curious high-necked blouse and her hair arranged on what was clearly some sort of frame so that it formed a halo round her head — something I remembered from old photographs at home — received me sceptically. 'I shall enquire,' she said in a pinched voice, 'whether Mr Halcro is free to see you.' He was free and indeed welcoming. 'Come away in,' he said. 'I was hoping you might find your way up these stairs one day. You see, I kent you were here. There's not a lot goes on in the University I don't know about.' He was a large man with a round, moon-like face, whose bulk was increased by a thick tweed suit of a curious yellowish-brown colour — what in our country dialect, using a farmyard metaphor, we would have called 'sharn-coloured'. He wore a stiff collar with a sober tie fastened by a pin on the head of which was a yellow cairngorm. There was little in his office beyond his desk, a bookcase with reference works and above his head a group photograph of some Scottish regiment. 'So you are Jessie Sutherland's son?' I had not expected him to use my mother's maiden name and remained mute. 'She was a clever lass, your mother. A great waste — a great waste.' It was not clear to me whether he was referring to her choice of profession, her marriage to my father or her early death. So I made a non-committal noise. 'And how is your father? Trouble with his sight, I hear. Well, none of us is getting any younger.' He pondered for a moment. I realized with astonishment that this hale middle-aged man was probably the contemporary of my half-blind, ageing father. 'And your Aunt Maggie?' he went on but did not give me time to answer. 'Very sharp she was in her youth and I expect not getting any less so.' He looked reflectively over the Firth of Forth to where the coast of Fife hid behind a rain squall. Then he turned his attention back to me. 'Now tell me what you're up to in Embro' town.' I said I was reading French and German with History as an option. He nodded approvingly. We were going to need people who were good at languages. For a lot of reasons. Business. Diplomacy. Of course I couldn't aspire to the Foreign Office. For that you needed the kind of finish they gave a young man at Oxford or Cambridge and he didn't expect my purse was quite as long as that. But had I ever thought of the consular service? A grand job. 'Let's see,' he went on, warming to the idea, 'with German you could be vice-consul in some place like Bremen or Koenigsberg. A very interesting job. Very. Ever thought of it?' I confessed I hadn't. 'Think about it, laddie, think about it. Getting to know foreign parts and ways — it broadens the mind. And of course there's always a job to be done — especially since that madman Hitler came to power — collecting information that might be useful to HMG in one way or another. Nothing spectacular — no John Buchan stuff — just keeping one's eyes and ears open. Think about it seriously — I would if I were in your shoes and had my life over again. If

21

you stick in to your books and get a decent degree you shouldn't have any trouble with the entrance exams and I'd be happy to give you a reference. Jessie Sutherland's boy should have inherited some grey matter.'

I thanked him although inwardly I felt the idea to be highly improbable. Then there was a silence in which I found myself wondering whether he had, as the saying went, been sweet on my mother. The thought troubled me, for I had not before thought of her in terms of sexual attraction. We both looked across to Fife where the rain was clearing off the slopes of Largo Law and a patch of sun rested uncertainly on its green shoulder. Suddenly, as I wondered whether I should now leave, he turned not, as I expected, to bring our conversation to an end but to embark on a new tack. What, he asked, was going on in student politics? What about the pacifists and the Peace Pledge people? I said there were a few of them about. On Armistice Day some had turned up for the two minutes silence in the Quad wearing white poppies they had got somewhere. 'From the Women's Co-operative Movement,' he interjected. There had been quite a scrap, I went on, with members of the Officers' Training Corps when they wanted to lay a wreath of them. I didn't think there was a great deal going on otherwise. I had been to a Unionist dance but that had been a bit cliquey. There was a Socialist Society and some people sold *Forward* in the Quad. In my year a couple of chaps read the *Daily Worker* and supported something called the Labour League of Youth, which seemed to be some sort of Communist organisation. Mr Halcro nodded. They were reading German like me and were going to refuse to spend their year abroad in Germany because of Hitler. Then there were the Scots Nats. They had hoisted the lion rampant on the dome of the Old Quad during the Rectorial election when their candidate had been a novelist with a big black hat and a tartan plaid. Mr Halcro laughed. 'Seamus MacGregor. The uncrowned king of Scotland. His father's an auld body that used to have a baker's shop in Brechin. Go on.' And then there was — I hesitated — Colin Elphinstone who said he was a

Marxist and had invited me to some sort of discussion group. 'Elphinstone of Usan,' Mr Halcro commented. 'A fine old family. He's a young gentleman having his fling. He'll come to his senses in a year or two no doubt, end up in the House in the Liberal interest, like his father. But I'd still like to know what goes on at these famous discussion groups. Mostly hot air, I imagine.' What really interested the people who had to take note of such things were the hard men, the dangerous, cold-headed ones, not enthusiasts like Colin Elphinstone, but people who used the chance of a university education and their bursaries to encourage social discontent. They were busy, for instance, in the National Unemployed Workers Movement, which was nothing but a Communist-dominated organisa-tion that exploited the ignorance of poor fellows who were out of work — for no fault of their own, mind you — and incited them to march on London and riot in Hyde Park. There had been attempts too to subborn the loyalty of soldiers of the Castle garrison. These had failed naturally and those responsible would, when apprehended, be dealt with. A few months hard labour in the quarries at Peterhead would teach them a lesson they'd remember for a while. But we shouldn't forget that lamentable mutiny — not so many years ago — in the Fleet at Invergordon when agitators got to work on the lower decks. Behind that sort of thing were twisted minds — often Jews, immigrants from goodness knows where — who wanted to destroy the fabric of society. He gave me a hard look and asked, 'Where do you stand — politically?' I said I was interested in politics in a very general way. If I voted it would probably be Liberal or Labour. 'That's all right, laddie,' he said. 'No one's saying a young man can't have generous feelings. Feelings are all right. But when the cards are down what matters is what people do. Now in the General Strike the students did a grand job — driving trams and buses down the Leith Walk and standing up to the toughs who tried to stop them. I was a special constable myself then and I saw that the spirit of 1914 — of the men who rallied to the colours then — wasn't dead.' He made a motion of his head towards the regimental photograph on the wall behind him. 'But what, I wonder, will those pacifists with their white poppies do if there is another war — which is not unlikely? If they and the hard men on the Left eat at the heart of the student body it will be a sorry day for Scotland and indeed for the United Kingdom. I can tell you that.' 'What about the Nationalists?' I asked. Mr Halcro laughed. 'Oh, they can go on having ceilidhs and playing the clarsach and shivering over peat fires in their cold Edinburgh flats. Wearing the white rose of the Jacobites — as if anyone cared — and making up a language out of Jameson's Scots dictionary to write poetry with. They may be daft but they're no danger. All they ever do is blether. Just blether.' 'Some of them say they can lay their hands on guns and dynamite. And there's talk of drilling in the Pentland Hills,' I said. 'Is that so now? Very interesting. I tell you, if there's any drilling its four men and a dog. But you wouldn't happen to know who these hot-heads are? Do they by any chance include a certain young man from Colonsay they call Callum Beg?' I nodded with astonishment and waited for him to go on. There was a long pause while Mr Halcro reflected once more, looking out to the Firth where a destroyer slid along through the rain to its base at Rosyth. 'Well, John,' he said at last, 'it's been an interesting chat. I like your approach to things. You're canny and you notice what's going on. How would it be if we arranged for you to drop in now and again — once a term maybe — or oftener if you have anything special to tell me. Even if it's only what goes on at young Elphinstone's study group. What I'd like from you is some idea of what's stirring and who the hard men are. There would be a wee fee for your labours. Shall we say a couple of pounds a time? We'll count this as the first diet and make it a bit bigger — to start you off like.' He rang a bell on his desk. His secretary appeared frostily with a dictation pad and a needle-sharp pencil poised. 'Miss Dalgleish, would you be so good as to let Mr Melville here have a five pound note on his way out. You will be seeing more of him, I expect.'

As I walked back to my digs I kept putting my hand into

my pocket to feel the thin paper of the five pound note. Where, I wondered, had Miss Dalgleish drawn it from? What was the nature of the fund over which she and Mr Halcro presided in their office in the severe streets of Edinburgh's New Town? What were the consequences of accepting the payment, for in this I agreed with my aunt that there is nothing for nothing in this world. Perhaps it was useless and unnecessary to enquire. If Mr Halcro was prepared to pay out good money for what you could pick up in the Old Quad or round a coffee table of students in some Princess Street store on a Saturday morning, why should I be too nice to take it? I could play the game so long as it suited me, then I would graduate — become vice-consul perhaps in some Hanseatic town on the Baltic — and leave the games behind me along with student life. But I was uneasily aware that things might not be as simple as that. I had been given a glimpse of a current of power running beneath the surface of everyday life. It was like the moment when, bearded and hirsute like his own tweeds, the owner of a wool mill had opened a hatch in the floor and showed me, a child of four, how the race of water roared towards the mill-wheel, dark, powerful and headlong, so that I started back and clutched my mother's skirt. From now onwards I would always be conscious of that underground force Mr Halcro had allowed me for a moment to glimpse.

Nothing in my upbringing had prepared me for Mr Halcro. I was, in fact, hardly prepared at all for life in the world, which throughout my childhood had seemed a mystery to me, full of reticences and secrets, of mysterious decisions, of inexplicable and frightening silences on the part of my father, shut off in his twilight, so blind that I had to lead him to church where I handed him over to the beadle who, in turn, brought him to the foot of the pulpit stairs. Then he felt his way up to his seat from which he rose and, finding the great red marker that dangled over the edge of the lectern, seemingly read the lesson for the day. I had gone over it with him earlier that morning after prayers attended by my aunt, my sister — a quietly rebellious girl — and the cook-maid, a relic of my mother's days, her face mottled from bending over the kitchen range. On weekdays she made mince or stew; for Sunday dinner, after the morning service, rice soup from which I fished with disgust pieces of leek and ranged them on the side of my plate. His sermons my father knew by heart. They were as dry as the Sunday roast beef. In this they contrasted with his impromptu prayers which were shot through with tearful piety. He never failed to beg us with a tremulous voice to remember those whom God in his infinite mercy and wisdom had taken from us and with whom we must hope to be reunited among the blest. This I took to be a reference to my mother whom I remembered as a warm soft presence who had taught me my prayers and sang in a low voice: *Shall we gather by the river/That flows by the throne of God.* Death proved, however to have little to do with shining rivers and much to do with a coffin on trestles in the bedroom where she lay with a curiously smooth face. I was afraid to look at her when my father lifted me up and long remembered with terror the feel of her cold cheek when, taking my hand in his, he made me touch it. She had gone to a happier place, he explained; but I was not convinced. Nor did anyone, from the tradesman to the old women who were the core of the congregation in the small cold church, seem to feel any joy at her passing over. Aunt Maggie, when she arrived to look after us, was hardly cheerful either.

The pattern of our lives was now set and no longer relieved by warmth and singing. Church was twice a day on Sunday with Sunday school after the morning service. In the cavernous church hall my sister stumbled over hymns at the piano. Our teacher was one of the elders who, in real life, had a small tailor's shop and made our uncouth clothes. By the time we were adolescent my sister and I were deeply agnostic, although full of clerical jokes. Question: Where is golf mentioned in the Old Testament? Answer: The Second Book of Kings, Chapter

26

9, where it says: 'Jehu drove furiously.' We also knew and could locate with great precision those dark texts about seed and issues of blood which no one would elucidate. By the time I went to University I had indeed been a Young Communicant and had taken bread and wine at the communion table, drinking unhygienically from the common cup. The wine was acid and the bread slightly stale. It was not an occasion that moved me spiritually. Once I left home I never again took part in the ritual.

There were those — mostly among his devoted lady parishioners — who considered my father to be a saint. 'Saint!' said Aunt Maggie. 'Soft they mean.' According to her he was putty in anyone's hands, was constantly overridden by his own kirk-session and a dummy at presbytery meetings. On the rare occasions when he took part in the debates he was heard out more for his blindness than for what he had to say. If she were in his place — and it was easy to believe her — she wouldn't sit there like a stook of corn and hold her tongue. So much was obvious from the way she dealt with the butcher and the grocer who had to face her when, notebook in hand, she went over the monthly account, disputing a ha'penny here and a penny there. The sharpness of her tongue was equalled by that of her sight which could detect a skimped piece of work, even if it were on the top of the roof, and spot dust on the most polished surfaces. It was an agony for my sister and me that in other people's houses she would surreptitiously run her finger along a ledge and secretly examine the tell-tale smudge on her glove. She had a wide knowledge of what she called 'goings-on' in the town, to which she referred by a code which it took me some years to penetrate. She and my sister in this connection shared secrets from which I was excluded. If they were talking together in the drawing-room the door would shut as I passed. If they were working in the kitchen, they and the cook, who was privy to such matters and no doubt a fruitful source of information, would fall silent and watch me go through to fetch my bicycle from the basement. Sometimes they would retreat to a bedroom through the door

27

of which I heard the sussuration of voices. Once, when I was twelve, my sister opened the door to find me eavesdropping. I had no supper that night and was forbidden to go swimming for a whole week. Had my father been a man at all, said my aunt, he would have taken a strap to my bottom. I had at such times a feeling of being totally alone in the world. I tried prayer but prayer did not help. I was left with a desire to know the unknowable, to see the unseeable, to pry at the riddles of life. The answer lay there behind closed doors, in whispers, in looks and glances interchanged by grown-ups, by my sister, by my aunt. I was drawn by a desire that was, I felt but dared not openly acknowledge it, linked to other longings, desires and fears. If now I was curious about Mr Halcro's mill-race and its dark power it was in the same way as I had long been curious about sex, wondering about it, speculating, advancing tensely towards the day when its mystery would be revealed.

On Bruntsfield Links I stopped to watch a group of middle-aged men in fancy dress — green jackets, green trousers and caps with what were supposedly eagle's feathers — shoot arrows inaccurately at large wicker butts: His Majesty's body-guard, the Royal Company of Archers. I had a deep contempt for such charades and those who play them. I had, in fact, no strong feelings of loyalty to anything — not to my old school, not to my father's church or faith, to the University or to the crown. Nor did I expect much from society. On one thing my father and aunt had been agreed. Once they had put me through university I would be on my own. 'I have enough to see your education finished with the help of your bursary,' said my father, 'but after that there's no use coming to me for subventions. I had none and you shall have none. And I have no connections. But you have a tongue in your head and some brains — so use them.' I watched the arrows droop towards the butts and the archers walk over to collect them from the ground. I felt the five pound note again. It began to dawn on me — in spite of my fears — that in Mr Halcro I did have a connection, which I perhaps owed to my dead mother. Through it I had become in some obscure way powerful, licensed to pry, to draw out secrets, to find the reality behind the play-acting of people like Colin Elphinstone, those favourites of fortune and birth. The pleasure would lie in concealing the power vested in me, even if by so doing I confirmed myself in my loneliness.

From that day on, although I walked about the Old Quad like any other boy from the provinces, losing my country accent a little, acquiring a certain knowledge of, in particular, German language and literature, I felt set apart as I embarked on an exploration of student politics. On Saturday evenings I was down on the Mound behind the National Gallery where the Communists and the Scottish Nationalists shared a shifting audience with a purple-faced crusader from the Church Army. In a pub opposite Mr Halcro's office I debated with ardent Nationalists just back from the Sorbonne, full of neo-Thomism and sophistical logic, whether a red rose might be said to be red in the dark. I went out collecting money for Republican Spain in gaunt housing estates and in the dark closes down the Royal Mile. In the Usher Hall — what Colin called 'the inverted chamber-pot' — I listened to the big names from London, the Red aristocrats, the Red clergymen, the Labour Party radicals and the Communist Party leaders, deploy their various modes of oratory in aid of the Spanish Republic — a cause that did touch me: which I felt to be permissible given Mr Halcro's comment about generous feelings. Wherever I went on the Left Colin was there, on familiar terms with the speakers whose names stood out in red letters on the notice-boards in the Quad, whether they were speaking in rented halls, in cinemas or at those smaller gatherings to which he began to invite me, calling me by my first name. It was as if the Spanish civil war had provided him with a stage on which to play a part, to exercise on audiences of all kinds from students to working-class men and women, the charm I had

29

noted from our first meeting. Now it was used to extract pennies, occasional shillings and even rarer notes to buy milk for Spanish children. Not that I believed him to be insincere when in the midst of his peroration his voice faltered with emotion; his passion was real enough — but so in a sense is an actor's. His sincerity came over too at the smaller meetings of his discussion group at his digs in a flat high above the Water of Leith. The walls were given a paradoxical gaiety by posters from the war: comical generals and cardinals sailing in a boat along with Moorish mercenaries to restore — as Colin commented ironically — Christian values; clenched fists grasping bayonets; initials — UGT, CNT, FAI, PCE; slogans — *No Pasarán!* One poster I remembered long after: a soldier in a long cloak on guard, the colours blue and grey, the slogan in what I took to be Catalan: *The nights are cold at the front.*

Gradually I began to identify the nucleus of regulars who prompted the discussion, asked questions when there was too long a silence and intervened to give what were defined as the correct answers. I began, too, to recognize their common phraseology: 'objectively speaking', 'subjective idealism' or 'bourgeois idealism', 'workers with hands and brain', 'petty bourgeois deviations', 'Trotskyist wreckers'. There was among them a young woman with small almost babyish teeth, reddish hair and freckles on her face and shoulders whom I watched with increasing interest, curiosity, tension and desire, as she tucked her legs under her skirt and, leaning forward on the floor with one hand, let her breasts fall forward into her blouse. Her name was Felicity, an upper-class name I had not come across before. Surnames were not used among the regulars, either as a social convention — they all appeared to know each other from London or Oxford — or as a security measure. She usually had with her — perhaps as an unconscious foil — Frederica, daughter of a member of the Central Committee of the Party, who took her name from Friedrich Engels. She wore sandals, was rather plain with long, slightly protruding teeth, a sallow complexion and great intelligence in her face. Sometimes I would catch her looking at me. Then she would turn her face away quickly and say something to Felicity. She rarely spoke but when she did her words had for her audience the authority of her father's political eminence. Often she had with her a man of about thirty: Brian Napier. He was almost bald with a sharp, pointed face and teeth stained with nicotine. What he did for a living was not absolutely clear. In talk after the meetings, in which he rarely intervened, although he would exchange whispered comments with Frederica, he hinted that he had done a certain amount of 'schoolmastering' at minor public or prep schools. He wrote it seemed and had even had something published in *Left Review*. In his company I felt ill at ease. He had a way of questioning that was like an inquisition. I was, I felt, being tested and examined. 'A very dark horse,' was Mr Halcro's comment. 'A very dark horse indeed. There are some gey funny things go on in these prep schools. Unmentionable really. I'd be interested to learn more of Mr Napier.' That I was eventually able to tell more I owed to someone I found more congenial: the young miner called Willie Moir to whom I felt myself closer in speech and accent, although he was unmistakably working class with his cap and his white scarf and his whippet, which he sometimes brought to meetings. Often we would slip off afterwards to a pub which was the howff of unemployed labourers, carters and young men of no occupation, past or present — like the one who claimed to make a living 'serving' a comfortable widow with a wee house in Comely Bank, or his friend who hired himself as fodder for flea-circuses. In such company, among the smell of wet sawdust, spilt beer and black rolled tobacco, we would mimic the English accents of the group we had just left and what we saw as their affectations. Willie's laughter had a slight anxiety to it, for the pub was out of bounds to Party members like him on the grounds that its regulars, being lumpen-proletariat (why are they called 'lumpy'? he asked) were liable with their cynicism and lack of political principles to corrupt the young and inexperienced. Besides it was close to Rose Street where the whores stood in the doorways ready to tempt clients up some

31

dark wynd. Did I know where Brian Napier did his drinking, though? asked Willie. 'You'll no believe this — but it's in an orra pub in the Lawnmarket — a recht midden o' a place — naethin' but wee hoors and sodgers frae the Castle.' It was a snippet of information that caused Mr Halcro to say: 'Well done.'

Willie had a sister, a stodgy, graceless, taciturn girl, called Agnes, who sat on the outside of the group, not taking part or showing any interest. She stayed on, however, when her brother disappeared without warning to join the International Brigade and die at the battle of Jarama. When the news came through she became in her grief a Madonna of the Left, approached with awe and reverence, tended by Colin and supported by him on platforms in school halls and trades union huts. If her grief was exploited it was no less genuine; her sorrow was inarticulate but deep. Tutored by Colin, I suspected, she was able to repeat a short speech of suitable phrases ending with the strangled shout of *No Pasarán!* The Madonna image was soon more than a mere figure of speech for she began to show unmistakable signs of pregnancy; whereupon Colin announced dramatically that they had been married in secret. 'That will take a bit of sorting out,' commented Mr Halcro. 'He must be daft.' But he was more interested to know whether there had been any attempt to recruit me yet. I said Frederica had indeed suggested that I should become a probationary member. I said I had been evasive. 'Quite right,' said Mr Halcro. 'These are deep waters. Keep them dangling till the long vac. Then you'll have your year abroad in Germany. A lot can happen in a year. Especially these days.' Our meetings were now firmly established and I enjoyed not only a regular fee but what Mr Halcro called a retainer — the immense sum of twenty pounds. I did not tell him that I was saving it up to travel to London that summer with Felicity. I had not mentioned her name to him nor naturally did I tell him that it was to her that I had recently lost my virginity.

It happened on a Left Book Club hike in the Pentlands. When she slipped on the path and twisted her ankle a little I volunteered to stay behind with her. She was quick to accept my offer. We rested among the high broom on the hillside, ate sardine sandwiches, shared our fruit-and-nut chocolate and laughed to think how, now that the sun was really high and the broom pods were crackling in the heat, the others led by Colin in khaki shorts would be sweating across the moors. She made no objection when I undid a button of her blouse and for the first time laid my hand on a woman's breast. After I had inexpertly made love to her she laughed and said: 'It's a good job I actually lost *my* virginity to a pony when I was in my teens.' She found my puzzled look comical and laughed anew: 'Riding can do that to a girl, silly, didn't you know?' So it was logical that we should arrange to go up to London together when term ended. There we drank China tea in a Chelsea tea-shop by the Thames called The Green Cockatoo, saw Soviet films in a Regent Street cinema, demonstrated in Trafalgar Square for the Spanish Republic, lingered in the Tate in front of Van Gogh's sunflowers and in some print-shop bought postcard reproductions of Franz Marc's blue horses. In front of a painting in the National Gallery of Tobias and the Angel we suddenly both had the same thought. 'Who does the angel remind you of?' she asked. Without hesitation, without prompting, as I looked at the fresh beauty of that Renaissance face, I answered: 'Colin, of course.' She gave me a curious look and smiled but made no comment. Then we went down to the country where her sister, Veronica, was getting married. There would be a spiffing party with the village band, a marquee on the lawn and lots of champers. I asked what 'the comrades' would think of it all; but she replied that family was family and the Party was something else. Her parents lived in Devon in a rambling house amid a mixture of gentility and squalor — antique furniture, family portraits, damp that peeled the wallpaper off the walls and mice-droppings in the larder. Her parents paid no more attention to me than they appeared to do to any of the other young men and

33

women, linked by parentage, education and class, among whom I felt strange and out of place. Felicity got into an argument with a young man who wore the badge of the British Union of Fascists with a certain bravado and announced that he was off to fight for Franco. Hitler, he announced, was a jolly good thing for Germany and for Europe, if it came to that, and we should damn well back him up. Felicity offered to push him into the lake but he was rescued and led off by a rather drunk, pretty boy who, to my astonishment, stroked his hand and put an arm round his waist. Felicity saw my surprise and laughed. 'I told you — to love me is (if I may coin a phrase) a liberal education. I'm sure, if I was a man, I'd find Colin Elphinstone irresistible.'

We slept that night in what must once have been a coach-man's house over the stables. Below us sat the family Morris, still ankle-deep in confetti, for the bride and bridegroom had driven to the station in it on their way to honeymoon in Juan-les-Pins, which — apart from being a super place — gave you a good chance of seeing the fighting just over the Spanish border. In the morning we lay and talked. Felicity was full of gossip about other members of the group. Did I know Frederica had a crush on me and was going to be fearfully jealous when she heard about us? I expressed surprise. 'Oh, you are naïve,' she said. 'She turns as red as a beetroot if you look her way. It's going to be really funny to see jealousy at work in a bride of the revolution, so to speak.' She went on to wonder what Colin was doing marrying that awful girl and getting her pregnant. It wasn't as if it were a question of love or even of lust — just a matter of political principle. An act of atonement for not going to Spain himself. Imagine marrying someone out of political principle! It was as bad as marrying for money. Brian? Goodness knows what he was, sexually — a neuter perhaps? But people who should know — people like my admirer Frederica — said he was terribly important and made all sorts of trips to France and Spain and Austria. Did her parents know? I asked. About her Party membership? Daddy was terribly upset, she replied, he would be — he was such a stick — but Mummy said that everyone should be a Communist at twenty and a Conservative at thirty. 'So I have a few red years ahead of me yet!' We parted in London. She was going to work for the Left Book Club. I felt deeply jealous at the ease with which she and her circle were able to pick and choose what they did while before me lay only the prospect of teaching languages in some Scottish provincial town — unless, of course, Mr Halcro and I got a consular job. Or there was a war, the coming of which I both feared and anticipated with a certain excitement. In the meantime I had my year at the University of Goettingen. 'You are a funny one,' she said on our last night together in her attic flat behind the British Museum. 'I wish I could make you out. Even when you're with me — even in bed — you're alone. You know what I think? I think you'd make a marvellous spy.' She fell back on the pillows laughing. 'John Melville, the famous agent. Tell me — have I guessed right? But I suppose your lips would be sealed.' She kissed me on the mouth and laid a leg across mine. She was killed in the Blitz.

Some of my summer doings I reported to Mr Halcro on my way through Edinburgh to Germany. He was not interested in young gentlemen going to fight for Franco. 'Quite unimportant,' he said. 'It's not the British way of doing things — dressing up for political ends. You'll see — the British Union of Fascists will fizzle out the moment war comes. Which it is going to do. But you'll see plenty of fancy dress in Germany. Churchill's right. We have to stand up to those cheapjack dictators. Even if it means war.' He was gravely silent for a moment. 'Interesting what you have to say about Mr Brian Napier. Who told you now?' I was conscious of a blush as I named Felicity. 'Fortescue,' he said, 'another good family. I expect she'll come to her senses too, don't you think?' I said I thought so too. Then to my relief he changed the subject. He had, he explained, a friend who was very interested in aeroplanes and wrote for a magazine called *Flight*. Would I mind

35

looking out for photographs of German planes for his friend's collection — pictures from newspapers or illustrated weeklies, that sort of thing. An original photograph would be even better, of course. Not that I should do anything silly taking one. Did I have a camera? No? Then I had better get one before I left — not too expensive — a box Kodak would do. I should let Miss Dalgleish have a receipt and she would reimburse me. As I rose to go he shook my hand warmly, retaining his grip for a second to say: 'Just a wee word in your ear, John. Girls and the kind of work you're doing don't always go well together. Ye ken the saying: Women are kittle cattle. The less they know the better.' He patted me on the shoulder and opened the door to the outer office. 'Miss Dalgleish, will you let John here have an advance on his retainer. He's off on his travels.'

In Goettingen that autumn I sat in the Rathauskeller and watched the water splashing at the foot of the fountain in the square. Beneath its elaborately wrought canopy the bronze statue of a goose-girl stood looking down at the birds she had brought to market. From their beaks a fine, clear jet of water fell into the stone basin. She was called, I learned, Liesl — something about which I teased her namesake, one of the Rathauskeller waitresses. She had the dark hair and brown eyes that I now knew meant she was probably a Rhinelander. On her day off she consented to walk with me in the beech woods and then gave further silent consent to mutual explorations as we lay among the sweet-smelling flowers of the forest floor. I showed off afterwards by quoting that medieval poem where the minnesinger says that broken flowers and grass betray the haunts of lovers. But she was not impressed. Hers was a sceptical presence in a society where the pastoral — boys and girls singing round camp fires — contrasted strangely with the military: the same young people marching behind their red and white banners with the black hooked cross and, at a sharp command, breaking into a chorus to which their feet kept pounding time. If Mr Halcro was right I might soon be fighting such boys, or those others from the town garrison who on Sunday afternoons flirted with the girls in the square to the music of the regimental band. I was a figure on the margin of this threatening pageant. I kept myself to myself, avoided political discussion and worked quietly at my assignment — a study of the influence of the Scottish ballad on German romantic poetry. To be a Scot, I discovered, meant to be exposed to jokes about wearing little skirts but also to be tolerated as being at least not English. To be English was to be basely commercial and at the same time immensely powerful — master of colonies, rival of Germany and obstacle to her *Lebensraum*. Some of this I heard from my landlord, a classics professor at the local gymnasium, who, perhaps because his marriage was childless, took an almost parental interest in me. Not a member of the National Socialist Party, although he shared its views on usury and the Jewish peril, he belonged to the German National Party and, more importantly in his eyes, was chairman of the local cavalryman's association; for he had seen service on the Eastern front in the war of 1914 and had taken part in one of that war's rare cavalry charges. His description was a set piece, shaped and no doubt embellished by years of telling and retelling, but one which conveyed strongly to me a strange and frightening feeling of excitement: the jingle of the harness in the waiting ranks, the slow move forward at the walk, then the canter and the trumpet call that levelled the lances for the charge, the growing roll of hooves. 'You know Latin, Herr Melville,' he said, 'so you will perhaps remember that great onomatopoeic line from Virgil: *quadripedante putrem sonitu quatunt ungula campum.*' He beat out the hexameter's lolloping rhythm on the table so that the beer almost spilt from his glass. He had, he explained, the highest respect for the British Tommy as a fighter — especially in defence — and in particular for the Scotsmen with their little skirts. Ladies from Hell, they had called them. On being transferred to the Western Front, alas in a dismounted role, he had found them a

37

worthy enemy. It was his earnest prayer that two sister nations might never again have to face each other across no-man's land when in the East there was an enemy of our common civilization and heritage. When he became excited in discussion the duelling scar on his cheek turned purple. Then his wife would appear from the kitchen, bringing with her a strong smell of sauerkraut, and beg him to be calm. She had a nut-brown face and greying hair accurately parted in the middle and pulled into a knot at the back of her head. She too was a fervent nationalist but had reservations about the Hitler Youth — all this camping with the sexes thrown together in a manner that must lead to immorality. There were, she said, terrible stories about Strength through Joy camps and holiday cruises for the workers. I was unwise enough to repeat the joke about the girl who lost strength through joy on the Lueneburg Heath. Her husband laughed but she withdrew coldly into the kitchen. Altogether hers was a chilly house; my bedroom was almost as sparsely furnished as my old one at home. On the walls were framed arrangements of dried grasses and flowers — edelweiss and gentian — which she and her husband had collected when walking in the Harz, and a yellowing chamois skull with delicate horns. Above the bed with its engulfing bolster hung a brown photograph of the unveiling of a huge monument to Hermann, the German warrior chief who had defeated the Roman legions somewhere east of the Rhine. One Sunday I brought home a bunch of white, sweet-smelling flowers picked in the woods and presented them to her with a formal bow. Like my aunt she could see through a gesture to the reality beyond; which was that I had picked them with Liesl after a pleasantly sensual afternoon in the woods. 'Waldmeister,' I said — woodruff — but my precise identification did not persuade her to give more than curt thanks.

It was the Sunday before a great civic and political event: a visit to the town by the Leader. From the back of the crowd by the Rathaus I saw him pass in his open black Mercedes, one hand extended in a frozen gesture, like the figurehead of a ship. I had with me the inexpensive box camera for which Miss Dalgleish's funds had paid. By the end of the day I had taken a number of snaps on the same roll that included pictures of Liesl holding the creamy woodruff before her breasts: one was of the Leader, another — but I doubted that it would come out — was of a flight of planes that came in low over the town and another still, taken from my bedroom window at the back of the house, of some tanks forming up on vacant ground before the parade. When, at the end of June 1939, my train approached the Dutch frontier and German officials, some in uniform, some in civilian clothes, came along the corridor I had a moment's panic, for I realized that Mr Halcro had involved me in something more risky than I had bargained for. But I passed without difficulty and on Dutch territory relaxed and laughed a little to myself.

When that autumn I called in on Mr Halcro on my way to an infantry depot in York he told me that his friend had been very grateful for the snaps and handed me back the negatives from which, I discovered on later inspection, the tanks and planes were missing although Liesl was there with her bunch of woodruff. I wondered whether Mr Halcro and Miss Dalgleish had been able to read the negative and if so what they had made of it.

I often wondered too whether it was Mr Halcro — or someone with whom he had connections — who arranged for my transfer from the infantry depot where I had been sufficiently obedient, neat and keen, to be promoted to the rank of acting (unpaid) lance-corporal. From there I advanced to full corporal (acting) and stood on the square to bawl and to shout and put the new recruits through the ritual of square-bashing. To my commands they marched and countermarched, closed and opened order, changed their kit and dress two or three times in a morning, stamped their boots, crashed their hands on the butts of their rifles as they saluted and, as a final demonstration of our joint skills, piled arms in tidy pyramids.

At the back of my mind — a memory I could not easily share with my fellow drill-instructors — was an image I recalled from some grandiose French painting of troops sleeping by their piled arms while the Emperor on horseback swept over their sleeping heads. I had to be content with the mute approval of the adjutant as he strode across the parade ground with his swagger-cane snapped under his arm.

When one cold morning in February 1940 I was ordered to report to company office, my first thought was that my skills were about to be recognized by secondment to a drill course at the Guards depot at Pirbright or, better still, by promotion to the substantive rank of corporal. Instead the company commander, a mild regular with a straw-coloured moustache, announced that I was to be posted forthwith to the School of Military Intelligence. 'Good at languages or something? Some sort of schoolmaster, were you? Well, we're losing a dam' good drill instructor. I had you down for Pirbright. I suppose you'll transfer to the Intelligence Corps. You know their badge. A pansy resting on its laurels.' He giggled. I saluted, did a smart about-turn and marched out with the company sergeant-major barking 'one two one two' at my heels. Next day I was in Buxton at the School, made up to sergeant and being drilled in military German by a refugee — a captain with duelling scars and a Jewish wife, who boasted he was the only person in the British Army to hold the Iron Cross Classes I and II and whose one real quarrel with Hitler was over his anti-Semitism. I became familiar with the nomenclature of the Wehrmacht and the SS. I studied the silhouettes, armament and performance of German tanks and planes and in the process recognized with interest the ones I had photographed in Goettingen. Little wonder that Mr Halcro's friend had been so grateful. I got to know the organization of the German army better than I ever would that of my own. I translated captured documents and signals intercepts. I was lectured on the interrogation of prisoners and what were referred to as 'psychological methods', including deprivation of sleep and interrogation in round-the-clock shifts. In what seemed a ridiculously short time I was commissioned and despatched on embarkation leave before sailing for the Middle East.

On my way north I visited Mr Halcro. He was strangely shrunk by the cancer that had suddenly matured and would shortly kill him. His tweed suit hung on him in a disconcerting way; his moon face had waned to show the outlines of the skull. He did not ask me for information — I had in any case none to give — but talked about the war and how to win it. With Churchill in command we would come out on top if we pulled our weight. A lot of these daft young men who had gone about with white poppies and selling Communist pamphlets had already come to their senses. I ventured to ask whether he had any doubts about a man, say, like Colin Elphinstone, who could get carried away by romantic notions and might do silly things. Colin Elphinstone, he understood, had been commissioned into his father's old regiment — which incidentally had been his own — and he gave a nod towards the photograph on the wall. No doubt he would have a very good war for he was officer material and a born leader, like his father who had got a Military Cross on the Somme. 'Patriotism will assert itself over political creeds — especially if they're acquired in one's youth.' He himself had said and done some pretty silly things before he enlisted and went off to Flanders. 'Mind you, I'm not saying there won't be problems when peace comes. But that's a long way off and I don't expect to be there to see it.' It was his valedictory. I tried to thank him for my posting to the Intelligence Corps but he feigned ignorance and dismissed my thanks with a wave of the hand. He died six months later. My aunt sent me his obituary from *The Scotsman*. When it reached me I was already in the Middle East. Naturally there was no reference to his mysterious connections and his fund — unless they were included under 'distinguished services in the national interest' for which he had been awarded the OBE.

It was on my way south from this meeting and from an uncomfortable farewell with my father, now alone with my aunt, for my sister had gone off to join the WAAF in the south, that I found myself on a train bound for King's Cross. In the corridors men slept on their kit-bags and cursed when others trampled across them on their way to the toilet. There was a thick fug in the compartment where we officers crowded tightly together on our seats and smoked or dozed under the blue light. I looked sideways at the young ATS officer beside me and thought I recognized the face under the cap. Yes, she said, she was Janet Munro. So we talked about people we had known at home. I asked her about Colin Elphinstone and told her the story about the ladder. She laughed and said Yes, Colin had had a crush on her and had once climbed up to tap on her bedroom windŏw but she hadn't let him in for the very good reason that her father was in the next room and a very light sleeper. Did she remember playing 'bear', I asked. She laughed. I could feel her leg warm against mine. Later in the semi-darkness, as the train groped its way towards London, we exchanged such intimacies as the presence of others and the cover of an army blanket over our knees allowed. On the platform of King's Cross Station in the bleak dawn she turned away with a faint smile and a 'Cheerio.' That was the last I saw or heard of her.

On the troopship I was able as a commissioned second lieutenant to look down from the wide, breezy spaces of the boat-deck, where officers, nurses and members of the women's services paraded, to the well-decks where the troops lay thick and sweating and the housey-housey callers intoned: legs eleven, sweet seventeen (and never been kissed), number ten — Downing Street, all the fives — fifty five. As orderly officer I went down between decks to check the brown stews that sloshed in the serving-pails to the roll of the boat and then made my way back to a five-course dinner through gangways packed with men who had queued for hours for an apple or a bar of chocolate at the NAAFI shop. I had, I reflected, much to be grateful to Mr Halcro for. Admittedly the corps to which I now belonged did not have the prestige or battle honours of my infantry regiment at York and was considered a strange and upstart body by the other officers on board, who wore smart regimentals, which even in the tropics had a certain licensed eccentricity about them: a coloured lanyard, a badge worn with a difference, odd collar patches. By them my corps was classed along with such menial outfits as the Royal Army Service Corps, the Ordnance Corps and even the Tank Regiment, whose members were notoriously mere mechanics and not cavalrymen. There were among them what I came to recognize as the tourists of war: sons of distinguished politicians, writers-at-arms, descendants of noble houses, who moved at will (or so it seemed) through the various theatres of war, sampling the excitement of a commando raid or a drop into enemy territory, moving on to where the action was picturesque and leaving again when boredom set in. I met them again later at General Headquarters in Cairo, where they looked in to gossip with donnish staff officers, their contemporaries at university or public school. They included Colin Elphinstone with his spell in the Long Range Desert Group and his drop into Yugoslavia where, to be fair to him, he was lucky to survive the desperate battle in the mountains of Montenegro as Tito broke out of German encirclement. But none of them knew the tedium of war, whether it was the endless combing through the letters and diaries of prisoners and the dead to find little clues which would allow those in the know to make confident statements about enemy strengths and intentions, or the patient waiting of the men in their weapon pits on the perimeter of besieged Tobruk in positions that were map references to be entered and logged in situation reports by people like myself, engaged on what Colin called the book-keeping of war.

I was sitting in the office where I laboured without distinction over the German Order of Battle and kept a huge card index on which I entered the names of the officers and non-commissioned officers of the German Africa Corps, its units and their strengths, when Colin came in — as the saying was — out of the blue: the stony wastes of the Libyan desert. His face had the curious parchment colour that comes from long exposure to wind and sun; his hair, his eyebrows, his shirt and shorts were impregnated with fine sand, which gave him a curious dusty look. He had come with information about enemy convoys on the coast road far behind the German positions and the fluid front of battle and had to wait — like any other of the uninitiated — outside the sanctum where my superiors handled that most secret of intelligence material: Ultra, the decoded signals traffic of the German High Command. As he waited I claimed acquaintance, and he remembered me with alacrity and no visible embarrassment over the circumstances of our last meeting — at a Left Book Club group where he had defended the Soviet-German Pact on the grounds that it allowed the Red Army to win space and time in the event of a Nazi offensive in the East; I did not remind him. Instead we talked with the ease common to such wartime meetings, when chance threw people together and allowed them for a brief moment to share certain memories from the time when life had been normal. It was from him now that I learned with a genuine pang that Felicity was dead. Then a staff officer emerged and, taking Colin a little apart to the big situation map, listened to his report. When he left we made a date to have a drink at the Turf Club next day. But that same afternoon I ran into him in a small bookshop in the centre of town which had a double reputation: one as the focus of some sort of Leftish activity and another as a place that kept not only a good selection of French literature but some interesting contemporary Egyptian writing in translation. Moreover the girls who served there were distinguished by their looks and intelligence. I had come to the shop precisely because I intended to ask one of them, an Alexandrine Jewess called Yvette, with whom I was becoming involved — heedless of security and undeterred by her possible politics — to drive out to the Pyramids that night. There would be a full moon under which, as I was guiltily aware (for such was the word from the

44

inner sanctum), the German tanks would be massing for a thrust towards the Egyptian border. If, as I hoped and expected, our moonlight expedition led to sex, it might be difficult to banish entirely from my mind the imagined sound of the enemy tank-tracks as they rounded the Eighth Army's southern outposts. But she was not there. Instead I found Colin, who had changed into his smart regimental trews, in discussion with the owner, a thin, scholarly-looking man, whose face had an ironical cast. When I walked in they broke off their conversation. Then Colin, turning to me with a smile introduced me — needlessly, for we knew each other already — to Raoul, the proprietor, who as usual was cool. There was something about the place that, from the first time I entered it, reminded me irresistibly of certain small bookshops I had explored with Felicity in London — bookshops closely linked to the Party to which she and Colin both then belonged. (Did he still? I wondered.) There was the same slightly conspiratorial air, the same diffidence towards outsiders like myself, the same mixture of politics and culture, with the latter acting as a form of cover. I made an excuse and left. Later that night I was dancing with Yvette, who had turned down the idea of a trip to the Pyramids, at Groppi's, the smart restaurant where officers, their mistresses and girl-friends, in and out of uniform, mingled with the *entraîneuses*, when Colin cut in and to the tune of *Deep is the Night* danced her off so effectively that she never returned. I left and consoled myself in an officer's brothel in the arms of a Maltese girl, who insisted on talking about her fiancé in the Royal Navy. But the memory of that evening stayed with me; it rankled. Next day Colin had vanished to where the armour clashed in the heat and dust.

It was when he came back to hang about GHQ in some vague capacity and wait for his chance to drop into Yugoslavia to Tito that he met Diana Pomfret Carter. Indeed I introduced them. The tall, blonde daughter of a major-general, she moved through the corridors of the headquarters building in the

45

elegant uniform of some volunteer outfit, for the ATS was socially beneath her, with a distant air which in part reflected the importance and high security status of the documents she delivered to the inner sanctum; for, unlike myself — at least at this point — she was 'on the list': one of the chosen few who knew the source of those amazingly accurate pieces of information which, in intelligence reports, were attributed to captured documents, prisoners of war and, more improbably, to agents. Colin had dropped in to consult my card-index and chat and was about to leave when Diana entered, and without so much as a knock walked into the inner office. Colin lingered, asked some vague question and fiddled with the card-index while he waited for her to reappear. When she did they exchanged over my head a glance charged with an explosive mixture of social recognition and sexual attraction. I made the introductions. Before they had left the room Colin had asked her with his usual nonchalance whether she would care to dine with him that evening. I did not hear her reply, for they were already in the corridor; but during the next weeks and months he became Diana's constant escort, to be seen with her at the Gezira races, drinking a John Collins on the terrace of the Mena House Hotel, or at slightly disorderly parties on houseboats on the Nile. When they were married it was naturally in St George's Cathedral. There was a guard of honour from Colin's regiment, pipers and a reception afterwards at the Gezira Club. The honeymoon was spent by the lake at Fayyum where officers from fashionable regiments spent their leaves duck-shooting. Shortly afterwards Colin vanished into the mountains of Yugoslavia, leaving Diana a cool grass widow.

But before that there had been an odd encounter in a café in a slightly out-of-the-way street where I used to go to watch the skill with which the customers manipulated the dice and shuffled the pieces on the backgammon boards. Here I came across Colin sitting at a table with a Signals sergeant. He expressed surprise at seeing me there and, without hesitation, introduced me to Tom Pressman, whom, he thought, I might have run across in civvy street. The sergeant looked at me curiously but there was no recognition between us. Then after a few minutes the two of them got up and left. It was no longer remarkable for a captain, which was Colin's rank, to be seen publicly in the company of an NCO; some of the old hide-bound patterns of army life were being eroded by temporary soldiers like Colin and myself, yet there was something strange about the occasion and about the speed and decisiveness with which they left me alone at my table. It was not until some weeks later that memory restored Pressman's face to me in a context: Colin's flat above the Water of Leith, the group with Frederica and Felicity, Brian Napier and someone introduced by Colin as 'Tom Pressman — a comrade from London'.

We did not meet again until the winter of 1944, when the Wehrmacht's final offensive towards Antwerp and the Channel was foundering in the snows of the Ardennes. It was in another headquarters — this time in Brussels where the flats we occupied and in which we worked, ate and slept were colder but had the same dingy squalor as the offices in Cairo, the same curious little dens where NCO's, encamped amid collections of pin-ups, performed their arcane duties. There once more I was sitting over the book-keeping of war when Colin came in, looking much older with a cast of sadness and fatigue in his face, as if he had experienced too much in too short a time; but the face of the younger Colin as I remembered it could still be distinguished, overlaid by the experience of war. He was now rather grand — a full colonel with the red tabs of a staff officer and a row of medal ribbons whereas I was still only a major with a couple of ribbons that merely said I had been in Egypt and Italy. As usual he greeted me with surprise and apparent pleasure and enquired what I was doing. I showed him.

Targets for Operation Veritable
LXXXVI Corps Administration HQ: Location RHEINBERG
1. Prisoners of war report that Admin HQ LXXXVI Corps,

along with the main Corps Supply Dump, is situated in the centre of the town of RHEINBERG.

2. Canadian Army is of the opinion that RHEINBERG is on the main supply route for the present battle. It is therefore a target that merits attention.

Targets: (i)   The railway station SW of the town at A208279
          (ii) A large supply dump in the centre of the town exact location unknown
          (iii) Road bridges across the ALTER-RHEIN at A211286 and A212288.

Attacks: Two attacks seem to be necessary
          (i) on the station
          (ii) on the centre of the town
          The latter would effectively block traffic on the two bridges mentioned.

Conclusion: In consideration of the importance of RHEINBERG as a supply and communications centre and the importance attached to it by Canadian Army an attack of a strength of up to 20 (twenty) bombers appears to be desirable at an early date.

'QED,' said Colin with a slight laugh. 'Who said the pen isn't mightier than the sword? I foresee a future,' he went on, 'in which wars will be waged by messages despatched from underground command posts. Just as many people will get killed — maybe more — mostly civilians. Meanwhile you're not doing badly. Keep it up, dear boy, keep it up!' He had in his hand a paper dart like the ones we used to make at school. A new model, he explained, invented in the otherwise boring department to which he had been posted on the grounds that he had to recuperate after his spell in Titoland. The paper clip in the nose, he went on, improved performance a lot. He launched the dart accurately through the office window and watched it swoop across the courtyard, rising and falling in the thermals from the kitchens, until it vanished into a window three floors below. 'My God,' he cried, 'I do believe it's gone in at the window of the Judge Advocate General. I should think it means a courtmartial. Conduct prejudicial to good order and military discipline — no, conduct unbecoming an officer and a gentleman in that on 20th December 1944 at about 11.30 a.m. he did launch a paper dart, which I now produce, which dart entered the office of the Judge Advocate General.' He made his exit in a flow of badinage and left me to my slaughter by memo. When next heard of he had contrived to be back with his battalion for the Rhine crossing.

We did not see each other again until some months after the German surrender, an event at which Colin was typically present in some capacity or other; he can be seen (just in picture) in photographs and newsreels of the German capitulation on that same Lüneburg Heath where the girls of the Hitler Youth had lost strength through joy.

By the autumn of that year we had got used to many things: to towns where rubble was piled like snowdrifts in the streets, leaving a narrow thoroughfare lined with caves and subterranean shelters labelled: Mueller Josef or Schmidt Karl; to the slogans of the Nazi times exhorting the nation to make a last effort for final victory now slowly fading on walls and hoardings; to blindworm trains nosing their way through wrecked sidings (to which I had added my mite of destruction) and to their passengers — many wearing the field-grey that was now the badge of defeat — who clung to the sides and roofs like swarms of insects; to the notice-boards at the stations — patchworks of handwritten or typed messages, often accompanied by a photograph: Who has news of Panzer-grenadier Foster Willy, 229 Pzgrenadierregiment, last heard of in Stettin? of SS Oberscharfuehrer Keller Johann last seen in Posnan? Who has seen my son, my father, my fiancé? We had become used to the strange feeling of moving among men and women who in defeat had a greyness and pallor, as if recovering

49

from collective shock, which contrasted sharply with my memories of the sunburnt marching boys and girls of Goettingen. We were familiar with an economy where chocolate and cigarettes were the true currency that could buy anything from a peasant's eggs to women, girls, boys. We had seen occasional survivors of the concentration and labour camps walking along the summer roads in their striped uniforms. Some of us had seen the women guards in their compounds, awaiting trial for the prolonged exercise of cruelties that it was difficult to relate to these pasty-faced, dumpy figures. We had heard stories — true? untrue? — but which in any case did not strike us as necessarily improbable of race horses shipped back to England in landing-craft; of V2 rocket-heads sent back for research stuffed with parachute silk; and more certainly — for who did not have them? — of personal reparations in the form of watches, books, binoculars, cameras, revolvers, bayonets, insignia. It was a time that increasingly involved the victors in the black market and its centres of corruption.

That autumn my office at the headquarters of the British Army of the Rhine looked depressingly on to a courtyard in the midst of which rose a pile of broken furniture, crockery, clothes, linen, books, rugs, personal trinkets, toys and family photographs. The first troops to occupy the little town had gone through the place with their usual thoroughness, had pulled the drawers out of the tables, dressers, dressing-tables and cabinets, and spilt their contents on the floor where they could more easily be picked over. Then when the flats were commandeered as offices the domestic débris had simply been shovelled out of the windows into the courtyard where it would lie through autumn and winter. I salvaged from the ruin a copy of Thomas Mann's *Magic Mountain* and a reindeer hat, sent back no doubt as loot from the Eastern Front. There was no more need for my card index; no more Ultra material to be kept in safes with secret combinations. The German

Army had come together like curdled milk in the flat lands of Schleswig-Holstein and then trickled away through the zones of occupation. Some people were said to be keeping a card-index of the Red Army units across the Elbe and Signals Intelligence were looking for Russian speakers. Meantime we were engaged — those of us in the group of offices round the desolate courtyard — on what was described as 'political intelligence', which was an amateurish attempt to gauge German public opinion. But at least it officially freed people like myself from the ridiculous rule of non-fraternization — which was being broken by all ranks for reasons that ranged from the business of everyday life to sex — and encouraged us to talk to the Germans, to listen to their apologies, to their attempts to divide the Allies, their tentative moves towards political activity. Sometimes it had all the marks of a ploy to keep us busy until demobilization came along. Meanwhile it allowed me to travel by jeep — now a privileged form of transport — all over the British zone and even down into American territory. In our own zone I would call in at the Field Security units in the countryside where the roads were lined with apple trees, so that I needed only to climb up and shake a branch for the bottom of the jeep to be filled with fruit. The Field Security officers lived like medieval barons with their comfortable quarters, their commandeered transport, their wine-cellars and their harems of blonde girls. At HQ we lived more soberly and envied those posted to Hamburg where life was said to be more colourful, more raffish. Naturally it was in Hamburg that Colin Elphinstone — as I learned — was stationed.

I do not know how he tracked me down to my office overlooking the dismal mound of rubbish, but one morning there he was in his Scottish regimentals, as vivid as ever, with an even more impressive row of medal ribbons. With him was a tall, gangling man of thirty-five or so with a boyish look although his curly hair was streaked with grey. His ill-fitting battle-dress had neither shoulder-flashes nor regimental badges. As Colin and I shook hands the stranger looked abstractedly out of the window. Then Colin introduced him as James Ashburton, whose work I no doubt knew. I did not but the name raised some vague echo from the frothy politics of pre-war days.

The point was this — Colin had to get James to Berlin. He was doing something for the BBC about German intellectuals and 'the inner emigration' — trying to find out whether there were interesting manuscripts hidden away in desk-drawers or other even safer places. Could I possibly find an excuse to swan up to Berlin and could they cadge a lift? He thought I probably had access to a jeep. I felt illogically, stubbornly inclined to resist this assumption of closeness, the way my collaboration was taken for granted. So I stalled and expressed wonder that Colin didn't have a jeep of his own, or at least a commandeered car; but apparently he had had no luck with transport; he was working at the Hamburg radio station and transport was quite simply tight. But if I really couldn't help he'd understand. It was a polite form of blackmail to which I capitulated so as not to embarrass further his gauche companion, who throughout sat and examined the toe-caps of his new army-issue boots with great concentration.

On the way to the crossing place into the Russian Zone at Helmstedt, Trevelyan sat in the back of the jeep. He saw with apparent indifference the gangs of ex-Wehrmacht men clearing the autobahn, the graves of the British and German dead by the roadside, the latter marked by little posies of flowers under their distinctive crosses, and the carcasses of tanks and self-propelled guns, stained by flames, jagged and dismembered, beginning to rust. He had an abstracted air, a kind of detachment, as if his thoughts were fixed elsewhere. So he was incurious when we made a detour to avoid a village where red and white flags flew over the roof tops: a colony of Polish forced labourers, awaiting repatriation, armed — people said — and living off the country like bandits. In the hills above the Weser Colin produced a map and guided us up secondary roads to an open space under a cliff face. We parked the jeep on some hard standing on a mound that overlooked a long, partly filled trench. There was a galleried entrance into the rock-face, long and low; beyond was a factory floor, intact, the machinery, the lathes, the assembly line still in place. We walked along the rows of machinery and wondered what they had manufactured — rocket parts? radar? secret weapons? — and who had laboured here. Colin went off to nose among a pile of papers and files in what had apparently been the works office. A safe stood open, empty except for an old-fashioned ledger with a leather spine and a marbled pattern on its leaf-edges. Colin carried it to a desk and opened it at random. There in a delicate clear German hand, using the Gothic script favoured by the regime, was a list of names — Russian or Polish or both. Before each name a number; after it the words 'Died — consumption' and a date. There were thirty or forty names to the page. The ledger was almost full. Stamped on the spine was the year: 1944. 'I'm taking it,' said Colin. 'You should really hand it in,' I objected. 'Balls,' he retorted. 'It will only end up on somebody's office floor. I know someone at home who will write it up. Let people know what it meant to be a slave labourer from the East. Plenty of people want to forget. Remember that Polish village we passed?' he said as we climbed in to the jeep, 'There are actually people who want to send in troops to flush them out.' As we drove off we looked down at the trench that held the dead.

At the crossing point the Red Army officer with his dark shadow of beard looked cursorily at our documents and signalled us past the sloppy sentry. We drove on for a little without speaking, then Colin turned to Trevelyan and said; 'Isn't it amazing — to think they fought their way here from Stalingrad on the Volga on the edge of Asia. Now they are here in the heart of Europe. It could be a turning-point in history.' 'It depends what you mean by a turning-point,' said Ashburton and fell back into silence. The long drive across the plains of the Mark Brandenburg with field after field of monotonous root-crops sapped conversation. But at one point it occurred to me to ask Colin how he had known about the underground factory. 'A German friend,' he said, 'a marvellous man — Schneider's his name, Hermann Schneider — you ought to meet him.'

Berlin astonished us out of our silence and made Colin exclaim when we saw the litter of the battle-field in the streets of a great city. We drove on through rubble where chains of women sorted bricks among the grotesque and fractured ruins. Ashburton looked about him with an air of bewilderment. I asked if he had known Berlin before. He nodded and peered at street names, looking for landmarks from another time. We deposited him at an officers' mess in an hotel near the Kurfuer-stendamm where he stumbled off upstairs in his ungainly boots to find his room and rest. Colin and I had a drink in the bar. 'Not a bad writer,' he explained, 'I knew him before the war — he was in the CP — who wasn't? — for about five minutes. Then in civil defence. At least he didn't bolt to the States like some others and write sanctimonious poems from a dive in Fifty-Second Street. But not the most cheerful of travelling companions. He wrote some good things about Berlin in the old days — before the war. Now apart from this piece he's doing for the BBC — you know, Culture, the Phoenix among the Ashes — that sort of thing — he's really looking for an ex-boy friend. He'll need to be lucky to find him. I should think he knows it. But it doesn't make him any easier to take.' Outside the Berliners came and went with an air of immense fatigue, dragging little trolleys laden with firewood from the parks and woods and oddly shaped bundles that might have been household goods, recovered or traded, or — since nothing seemed improbable in this desolation — the body of a small child on its way to burial. Old women trudged by with bags on their shoulders. In a side street opposite the mess younger women in curious felt hats with feathers that made them look like raffish Maid Marions offered themselves to the passers-by. We waited and drank another whisky. It was on the tip of my tongue to pick up the half-mocking reference to membership of the Communist Party, but the days when I had used to pass on political gossip to Mr Halcro seemed immensely distant among the ruins of the enemy capital whose fall had felt like a line drawn across our lives. So I enquired instead why Colin was working at Radio Hamburg — I had thought it would be film, given his interest in that sort of thing. 'No such luck, dear boy,' was the reply. 'There is no film industry and if there were it would be in the American Zone. So I settled for wireless.' I should come to visit the studios. The Germans had this amazing invention: recording on magnetic tape. It was going to revolutionize the reproduction of music — think of it — no more discs, no more scratchy needles. Just the slight hiss of tape.

When Ashburton at last appeared it was with a list of addresses he wished to visit. Colin offered a Scotch — it was refused — and suggested we wait till next day for it was already late afternoon. But Ashburton was stubborn so we drove him to Schoeneberg where he told us to stop in front of a villa which rose, amazingly intact, among the suburban ruins. We watched him clump up to the front door, ring and disappear inside. Colin was quickly impatient in a lordly way and muttered about not being merely a driver. I reminded him that I was the driver if anyone was. He became moodily silent. Suddenly Ashburton appeared and beckoned us into the house where, in a room filled with handsome books and with its furniture and ornaments apparently unscathed, he introduced us to a tall grey-haired woman of about fifty. She had a fine but hard face that for want of a better word I would have called Prussian, and her daughter had the kind of dark hair and brown colouring that reminded me of my goose-girl, Liesl. Ashburton's German was rusty and painfully anglified but he managed to introduce us to 'an old friend from before the war, Frau von Wartenberg, and her daughter, Helene, who is an actress'. We exchanged a few stiff remarks in German into which Ashburton broke to explain that the ladies had been telling him about the behaviour of the Red Army troops. A tale of loot and rape, he said. Colin remarked sharply that there didn't seem to be an awful lot missing from this room and added icily that, having himself seen a few German atrocities, he hadn't come to Berlin to listen to atrocity stories from Germans. Ashburton might like to show the ladies the ledger which was still lying in the jeep. The two women looked impassively from speaker to speaker; it was impossible to tell from their faces how much they understood. I said to Ashburton that we would be back in an hour's time and led Colin out. Standing by the jeep he kicked the tyres in a rage. 'You must know,' I said, 'that there's a lot of evidence about rape.' 'I will not,' he shouted, 'listen to Germans accusing Russians of atrocities! What about Auschwitz? What about Dachau?' What had Ashburton's friends said or done when the Germans were looting their way through Eastern Europe and piling the corpses in the mass graves? How did we know what it felt like for Russian soldiers when they liberated the death camps, opened the graves or found camps full of starving Russian prisoners of war? In any case didn't all armies loot and rape? There were some odd stories about American GI's. And what about that pile of stuff in the courtyard under my office window? He walked off through the empty streets with the ledger under his arm. I drove around a little through suburban villas pockmarked by bullets and shrapnel. As I stopped to watch an elderly couple pick through the rubble and extract pieces of broken furniture, a boy of thirteen or fourteen in what might once have been a uniform approached: 'Hey, Joe,' he said. 'You American? Du — Zigaretten?' He looked suspiciously at a small packet of NAAFI cigarettes. 'Nix good,' he commented but pocketed them just the same. 'You want girl?' he went on. 'I got girl. Nix weit. My sister, sixteen. Forty cigarettes. OK?' I remembered how in their poverty the ragged children of the Cairo had touted their sisters; Colin, I felt, should have been there to savour the depths of defeat. I shook my head and drove off slowly. The boy ran after the jeep shouting. I accelerated and he stopped in the middle of the road, swearing loudly. When I got back to the villa Ashburton was standing on the pavement. 'Where is he?' he asked. 'Colin? Oh, he got tired of waiting,' I replied. 'Does he know,' said Ashburton after a silence, 'that the daughter was raped three times and the mother twice?' I said I supposed not and we drove back in silence to the mess.

56

That night Ashburton was distant. He would eat in the mess, he said, and then do some work. With Colin I drove over into the American sector where I had some friends from Army Intelligence — a New York lawyer and a couple of academics who had been 'on the list'. The food was better than it would have been with Ashburton, the Bourbon plentiful and the company congenial. Colin was persuaded to talk about Yugoslavia and the partisan war, which was a safer topic than the behaviour of the Red Army in conquered Berlin. As he spoke there was a pressure of feeling behind his words, contained but perceptible. From time to time he stopped and collected himself before going on, stubbed out a cigarette or took a sip of whisky to cover what might have been a tremor in his voice. He spoke of the casualties left with their nurses in camouflaged caves — maimed, blinded, desperately wounded or sick with typhus — each with a few rounds of ammunition and how the Germans and their allies, the Chetniks, tracked them down to shoot them where they lay. His stories of killings and revenge, of courage and cruelty, were very different from what the rest of us had known as war with our files, card-indexes and little safes for secret documents. 'Well,' said the New York lawyer, half joking, half embarrassed by the tension, 'it will make a great film.' 'I'm glad you think so,' said Colin bristling. 'I mean,' the lawyer went on unperturbed, 'this war is going to be a gift to Hollywood whether we like it or not.' He paused. 'Did you ever wonder,' he went on, 'what sort of trouble you were storing up for the future down there in the Balkans?' 'I knew,' Colin answered, 'to speak in purely military terms, that if Tito lost, a lot of German troops would be available for the defence of Hitler's Fortress Europe or to fill the gaps on the Eastern Front. Let me remind you that Churchill — who was hardly a sentimentalist — backed Tito.' 'I think there are a lot of things — a lot of official policy — that we are maybe going to regret,' the lawyer continued calmly. 'I think for instance, and just for the sake of argument, that perhaps instead of disarming the Wehrmacht we should have turned them round and got them to send the Russians back where they belong.'

At this point I said we had better be getting back, we had a long drive to the British sector and it seemed the streets weren't always too safe at night. They were, in fact, almost entirely empty. Occasionally a jeep-load of military police drove screeching through the chicanes of rubble and loose stones. Just off the Siegesallee we turned a corner and almost collided with a Russian truck lying on its side beside a crashed petrol bowser. The truck's engine was still running. Two men lay groaning on the asphalt. A trickle of petrol spread towards them. A couple of dazed Red Army privates sat on the pavement and watched. Colin jumped out. 'Get them clear before it all goes up,' he shouted and dragged the injured men to one side. One was an officer bleeding profusely from a head wound; he smelt powerfully of liquor. 'We've got to get them looked at,' said Colin. Between us we loaded them into the back of the jeep. As we drove off the two privates unslung their tommy-guns uncertainly but did not fire. So began a prolonged tour of hospitals from which authority in one form or another turned us away. There was a deepening pool of blood in the floor of the jeep. After the last refusal Colin climbed out of the jeep just as I was about to drive off. He ran up the steps again and pounded at the door. A frightened nun opened. Colin shouted at her. A doctor came running downstairs followed by either the mother superior or the matron. 'You will take these men at once,' Colin shouted in German. 'That is an order!' The doctor objected. It was a private clinic. They did not treat Russians. Colin shouted louder. Reluctantly the matron summoned a couple of orderlies with a stretcher. The Russian officer was by now very pale, his arms dangled as they lifted him. His companion could just scramble out of the jeep and crawl up the steps. 'Drunk!' said the matron with distaste. 'Then at least,' said Colin coldly, 'you won't be able to say they raped you.' She slammed the door in our faces. As we drove off Colin took a deep breath. 'I shouldn't have said that. I try not to be prejudiced against the Germans. But by God they try my temper sometimes. You know the

58

way they go on. Me? I was never a member of the Party! Bin nie PG gewesen! Where did all the Nazis come from then, I'd like to know? All these women and girls hysterical with excitement, all the men and boys lining the streets, shouting, screaming. And what about your American friend — happy to contemplate fighting with these people on our side! What I should have told him was that but for men like that Russian officer — pissed out of his mind and all — we wouldn't be walking about free men today. I can tell you one thing. I didn't fight in this war to end wars to end up in some sort of anti-Russian crusade led by Uncle Sam. No sirree!'

I saw him again in Hamburg on my way back to England to be demobbed. At the radio station he showed me round the studios, demonstrated tape-recorders with great facility and talked about microphones and acoustics. He had a very grand flat overlooking the cold waters of the Alster with a grand piano and an imposing array of books. It had belonged to a Nazi lawyer, now in custody, who appeared to have bought the books — complete sets of Goethe and Schiller and an assortment of classics — by the metre for they were unopened and unread except for certain curious works on 'the history of morals' with more or less pornographic illustrations. No doubt, said Colin, he would in due course be ticked off by a denazification tribunal and allowed back to his practice after some trifling and temporary restriction of his civil rights. He had himself got to know one or two really remarkable Germans — the kind the members of the Control Commission who were supposed to be leading Germany back to democracy didn't come across much — or pay much attention to if they did. Such as? Such as an old docker who had taken part in the Hamburg rising of 1923 and had survived prison and concentration camp in the Third Reich. He was a member of the Anti-Fascist League which, it was notorious, the Allies simply ignored. They preferred neutral specialists who went on doing the same jobs as they had done all along under Hitler — or else

59

safe and generally right-wing politicians from the days of the Weimar Republic, whom they dug up in the most unlikely places, dusted off and installed as burgomasters and so on. Then there was a guy called Hermann Schneider whom he had managed to find a job for at the radio station. Not without difficulty, he might say, because Schneider was considered politically suspect. Why? Because for a time he had been a member of the German Communist Party in the 1930's — something he had paid for by service in a punishment battalion on the Eastern Front and had been lucky to find his way back to Hamburg in those confused last days of the war, when the Field Gendarmerie were stringing deserters up on lamp-posts in an attempt to stop the final rot. I expressed surprise that he hadn't stayed in the Russian Zone to which Colin replied in his rather haughty way that he didn't see why there couldn't be a place for men like Schneider in the West. But I would see for myself because he was coming round to the flat later. Meanwhile he had a treat in store for me. He was going to take me to the opera. I said I wasn't a great one for opera. I had only ever seen things like *The Mikado* done by the operatic society at home. He laughed and said he remembered the performance where half the fun had been recognizing the butcher's son as the Wandering Minstrel. And Janet Munro, I said, as one of the three little maids from school. 'I'd forgotten that,' he said and went on without further reaction to explain that this was something rather different: the first performance of Beethoven's *Fidelio* since the fall of the Third Reich. The director was from the radio station — a very bright, politically sound chap with an excellent record for non-co-operation with the Nazis in the cultural field. It was bound to be an interesting occasion.

That evening we found ourselves in a bitterly cold hall with a makeshift stage at one end and the orchestra deployed on the floor in front of it. The audience was entirely German; they looked at us curiously, trying to disguise their interest. Colin wondered, whispering behind his roneoed programme, what they had all been doing two years, or even one year, ago. They had about them that pinched, dowdy air, that sallowness of complexion with which the Occupation had made us familiar. When the music began the players seemed to have trouble in finding their pitch; the wind instruments, in particular, fumbled around the notes in a way that made Colin shake his head impatiently and mutter about the damned cold. Some of the music I recognized — the trumpet call in the overture, for instance — because Felicity had had a record of it which she played obsessively and said it sent shivers down her spine. She did not know the rest of the opera and could not tell me anything about the plot. Following it now I found it tiresome and improbable. The heroine, got up as a man to look for her imprisoned husband, was dressed like the principal boy in a provincial pantomime — another of my rare theatrical experiences — except that her legs were nothing like as good. But one moment I found both eerie and frightening. It was when the prison-doors opened and to a chorus that rose and swelled, the inmates came groping into the open air and the light of the sun. As they emerged a gasp went through the hall. The prisoners wore the striped uniform of the concentration camps in which we had seen them trudging home in the first days after the surrender. 'My God!' said Colin as we left the building, 'that was a moment I shan't forget. Isn't it exciting to see great music make a political point like that?' I objected that it wasn't so much the music as the costumes that had made the point. Maybe, he admitted, but it was still a political gesture requiring considerable courage to have it in the scenario in the first place. Anyway *Fidelio* was thoroughly and consciously political. Did I remember that piece of dialogue — admittedly not sung but Beethoven had retained it — where the wife says of the prisoner in the deepest dungeon, who is of course her husband, that he must be a great criminal and the gaoler replies: 'Or else he must have great enemies.' 'I find it,' he said with one of those sudden bursts of enthusiasm that caused his cheeks to flush and his voice to shake slightly, 'I find it absolutely marvellous!'

As we spoke we hurried back through the bleak streets to the flat where the temperature was only slightly higher than it

61

had been in the hall to wait for Schneider. He turned out to be a man of about the same age as Colin and myself — in his late twenties. His face was a curious light brown that had nothing to do with health and the sun; it was deeply lined; his hair was almost white. Conversation proved to be difficult. Perhaps he was merely guarded in the presence of a stranger. At all events he did not have much to say for himself. Yes, life in a punishment battalion had been hard. They were used for clearing forward minefields. Yes, he had been at Stalingrad but they had been moved to another part of the front just before the Russian pincer-movement closed round it. Yes, he had been at Kursk. And at Orel. Yes, there were a lot of Nazis around. They were coming back into the open — the little ones at least. At the radio station, too. Most of the British officials had ridiculous ideas abour fairness and wouldn't get rid of people who were more or less compromised. We drank a little and talked about the opera. The director was a friend of his. He had survived a spell in Neuengamme, the concentration camp just south of Hamburg. We would hear more of him. When he had taken his leave, which he did with great formality, I asked what was wrong with him. Colin was quick in his defence. What was wrong with him was that he had had a bad time under the Nazis and a difficult time — to say the least of it — since the surrender. But he was really very interesting. 'I think he will probably write something good. Ashburton should have met him instead of those inner emigrés he was searching for in Berlin. And he is a splendid broadcaster.'

We had a parting drink at the bar of the Vierjahreszeiten, now an officers' mess and thronged with military personnel awaiting demobilization, civilians in Control Commission uniforms, journalists and official sightseers. Colin looked around with distaste. 'Imagine how many people were killed or fucked up for life to make this possible.' I commented that for a man of the Left he took a rather lordly view of things. 'But don't you find it seedy?' he argued. 'All these insurance salesmen and country-town solicitors with RAF moustaches and RAF slang trying to impress the ladies of the Control

Commission with stories about how may Jerry fighters they pranged. And those Control Commission types who naïvely think you can export the British political system — right down to local government — and the British broadcasting system and would rather have the little Nazi they know than someone who was in the camps but might be a Red.' He reflected for a while, looking through the cigarette-smoke to where a tall blonde officer brushed his Guardee-type moustache with the back of his hand with a studied gesture and, raising his glass, looked fixedly at the legs of the young woman on the stool at his side. 'I don't know about you,' Colin went on, 'but I think we are going to take more back to England with us than the odd dose of the pox. It's going to be the legacy of Cairo and Naples and Hamburg, of the black markets and the brothels — the idea that anything at all in this world can be bought. It will come home with the troops and with the hangers-on and it will work its way into the heart of British society like a canker.' Wasn't it some comfort, I enquired, for him to know that there was a Labour Government? He agreed. At least there wouldn't be the dole and unemployment like before the war. There might even be a bit of social justice. Fair shares for all. What was I going to do when I was de-mobbed? I said I had really no idea except that I didn't feel like teaching. Which was all I was really equipped for. He demurred. With my experience in Intelligence there must be openings. Journalism? the Civil Service? or what about — ? Here he laughed so loudly that people at the bar turned their heads to look our way. 'What about,' he said, recovering himself, 'one of the security services? MI5, say?' He laughed again and ordered another drink before going on to say by what struck me as a curious process of association: 'Do you remember Brian Napier? Poor man, he did a spell inside for inciting the garrison of Edinburgh to disaffection — or something equally improbable. I know he used to drink with the Jocks in some terrible pub in the Lawnmarket. But frankly I thought he was merely interested in the rough trade. Anyway he now runs some sort of secondhand bookshop off the Strand. You should

63

drop in if you're in London. He's got the most amazing connections in Fleet Street and thinks he can get something done with that ledger we found with Ashburton. Poor old Ashburton, he didn't like me much, did he? Probably because I know too much about him and some of the terrible agitprop stuff he wrote in the heyday of the Popular Front. To be spoken by Young Communist choirs! He really was looking for an old boy friend in Berlin. Touching. He didn't find him because he had died in Belsen — and there was nothing in anybody's desk drawer. Sad!'

My demob leave took me through Edinburgh, where the Old Quad was full of students of my own age or slightly younger earnestly catching up with degrees. The group Colin had belonged to was completely dispersed. I wondered how many of them were still to the left of the Labour Party in these their maturer years. I had a dram for old time's sake in the out-of-bounds pub and took the train north in my demob pork-pie hat, my brown demob sports jacket and my demob flannels. I found my father almost totally blind and living in cold discomfort with my aunt. She was as waspish as ever, found her scapegoat in the Labour Government — she fully expected that I had voted for them against Churchill but then some people had no gratitude — and imagined I'd be off south, wouldn't I, leaving them to fend for themselves in their old age. For my father's sake — if not for hers — I ought at least to look for a job north of the Border. After all my sister was away in the States with that American husband of hers whose name my aunt couldn't pronounce, sending food parcels. Fancy that — the Americans sending us food parcels! It just showed the pretty pass the Labour Government had brought the country to. But to come back to my intentions, she took it that it would be too much to expect that I would bother to make the effort to stay away from London. Because she knew that was where I would end up. I'd always been itching to get there. That last summer before the war when I had simply disappeared down south — goodness knows how I had been able to afford it and goodness knows what I had been doing and in what company. She had her suspicions. But what did I care?

My father sat over a miserable fire and fingered the edge of a tweed rug he had over his knees with long white fingers. He had grown immensely pale, almost transparent. His head shook persistently — not violently but gently and irritatingly, so that every now and then my aunt would say sharply: 'Willie, I wish you would stop wagging your head.' Then the rhythm would falter for a second or two before starting up again. A deep chill pervaded the house and pursued me into my rock-hard bed in my old room, where the cupboard was still stacked with my schoolbooks and adventure stories by Henty. I managed to last out a week, nipping off regularly to a pub in the High Street, which I entered surreptitiously with a sudden side-step that made me vanish before the eyes of anyone walking behind me. In the High Street I looked at the young married women with their prams and wondered if I might recognize in one of them a girl from school or even from 'the berries', pushing babies sturdy on wartime codliver oil and orange juice. My school friends were scattered. One was dead at Alamein; another waited to be demobbed in the Far East somewhere: yet another was a doctor in the Outer Hebrides. The rest I could not trace. When the time came to leave I went in to where my father sat. He turned his head in my direction at the noise of my entrance. 'Well, Father, I'm off,' I said and took one of his cold hands in mine. There was a slight answering pressure from his fingers. He nodded his head and moved his lips a little perhaps in benediction. No sound came from them. I turned and left the room. I knew I should not see him alive again but did not greatly care.

PART II

On the train south I turned over the options in my head. Before I left Germany our brigadier had sent for me to make an offer. I could stay on in Intelligence, he explained, with the substantive rank of captain — everybody was going to have to come down a peg in peace-time, he explained with a wry smile — and carry on with the kind of work I had been doing. Order of Battle. Of the Red Army, naturally. Papers on enemy intentions, stuff like that. Not quite as exciting as the dope I had been handling, but we had to get down to some solid work on Russian formations, strengths, personalities and so on. There were one or two ex-Wehrmacht types — but I was please to keep this under my hat, for obvious reasons — very good chaps they were, too, who were prepared to pass on what they knew. And they knew a lot. Or if I felt I had had enough of army life — which he would quite understand — I could have a civilian job at the War Ministry working for the Joint Intelligence Bureau and do much the same sort of job. I had said I'd think it over which was a polite way of saying No, for I was bored with high-grade clerking and wanted a change; when I got back to London, I determined, I would ring up Peter Baillie, who had been high up in Field Security and had said to call him any time. Such offers, I knew, did not necessarily mean much, particularly when made at a drunken farewell party in an officers' club at HQ British Army of the Rhine. So I waited a little before calling. Meanwhile I had installed myself in an Earl's Court flat with Jennifer, an ex-WAAF, who had had something to do with Special Operations and was, in a manner of speaking, widowed, for her French boyfriend had gone back to Paris and there disappeared. When

I did ring Baillie there was a suggestion of hesitation in his voice, but I hung on and at last he invited me to lunch in his club, which was very brown, brown portraits on the walls and rows of brown volumes in the library where I sat to await his arrival. When he came in I was struck — as I constantly was at this time — by how much of their authority people shed with their uniforms and badges of rank. Without the red collar patches of a staff officer, the insignia of a full colonel and a row of medals, he looked like any middle-ranking civil servant; which is precisley what he was. Something in the Home Office, he gave me to understand, without being very specific. He called me 'old man' and put on a show of friendship, an old comrades' act which was not totally hypocritical: it was merely that the terms of reference no longer applied now that he was back with his ambitious wife in a smart square off the King's Road. 'At least it's not whale steak,' he remarked apologetically over the main course, which was immensely tough, 'and the wine's drinkable, don't you think? The cellar's not bad. Jolly good, in fact. You should join. I tell you what — I'll put you up for membership, if you like.' This time I knew the offer was not to be taken seriously. In any case I preferred the drinking club run by an androgynous creature called Grace to which Jennifer had introduced me — just off Fitzroy Square and, unlike some other places not overrun by characters with RAF-style handlebar moustaches and ex-Desert Rats with sand glued to their boots. After the meal we sat a little apart from where members snoozed or read their papers. Our coffee table was in an alcoved window that gave on to a melancholy patch of flags and sooty shrubs. The afternoon sky was smudged by sleet showers. 'I'm very glad you rang,' he said, not altogether truthfully, once the coffee and port had been served. 'It so happens that since we spoke I have heard of something you might like to consider. I chance to know — don't ask me how — that before the war you did some rather useful work in Edinburgh for poor old Halcro. I think I may say that I can make you an offer. Which is this. If you felt you could carry on on the same lines, providing the odd bit of gen when it comes your way, you could have a retainer — not a princely sum, I admit, but adequate if you supplemented it — and no doubt you could do with something to mitigate the rigours of civvy street. It wouldn't necessarily interfere with any other plans you might have in mind. You needn't give an answer this minute but if it's Roger and Out — so to speak — just report to this address,' he passed me a typewritten slip of paper, 'and say the magic word, as it were, they'll put you in the picture.' I said I'd think it over. 'Jolly d.' said Baillie. 'By the way, have you anything else in mind?' I said I'd thought vaguely of journalism. 'Why don't you ring Ewan Campbell at the BBC's Overseas Services — he's terribly nice and helpful — say I told you to ring. It's not as romantic as it once was — all those coded messages to the Resistance — *les sanglots longs des violons* — that sort of thing — but I expect they could use a German speaker. Now I simply must dash. We ought to meet more often.'

I considered his offer by the pond in St James's Park, where the ducks cruised among moulted feathers and dead leaves or hydroplaned to where a small girl with a nanny cast her bread upon the waters. A man and a woman sat on a bench talking quietly and looking intensely into each other's faces. They were in their forties — civil servants perhaps, discussing the shifts and mechanisms of adultery over their sandwiches. I followed them when they left, walking back towards Whitehall. They parted with a lingering touch of the hands, then hurried off in different directions with heads bowed against a whirl of sleet. Trafalgar Square was empty and the pigeons disconsolate. I took shelter in the National Gallery. In front of the picture of Tobias and the Angel I thought of Colin and Felicity, and how their birth and breeding had allowed them to play at politics like Marie Antoinette playing at dairy-maids. Poor Felicity was dead; there was a bomb-site thick with willow-herb where her flat had been; but Colin was alive talking the politics of the heart, which might be harmless — might also be more dangerous in this post-war world where the enemy order of battle was that of the Red Army. No doubt he would

71

effortlessly find some new incarnation in civvy street. Certainly although not all that rich, he would not have to worry, as I did, about a dwindling demob bounty; which was why Baillie's offer began to present itself as a tempting life-raft — something that would allow me to look around, try journalism, ring Baillie's friend at the BBC. I knew that if I did decide to accept Baillie's offer and speak the magic word at the address in my pocket, I would be letting myself in for the kind of game I had thought I had abandoned when I was called up and bidden to report at the infantry depot in York. As luck would have it, I had not really got away from these games which grown-up men like Mr Halcro played in deadly earnest — games the business of war had made respectable: games of deception, games of detection, games of information and disinformation in the playing of which the lives of men were staked and lost. On the other hand I also knew how little real importance one should attach to much of their activity which involved a great waste of time and energy and human resources. I had seen sections of a headquarters staff collect information squirrel-wise and refuse to pass it on to others who might have fitted it into their own particular jigsaw and even made use of it to influence operational decisions, because in its possession lay power, mystery, access to the counsels and ear of the great men who determined the course of a battle, a campaign, a war. I had no reason to believe that in peace-time things would be much different. Besides what could I know or learn that would be useful to my new 'Mr Halcro' — at most some bits of gossip, a name, an address, perhaps, snippets overheard, nothing substantial but apparently worth good money. Why should I not give it a whirl? On my way out of the Gallery I found a phone-box and rang Jenny at the flat. We met at Grace's. Even among her oldest customers there were doubts about Grace's sex, which they would discuss with new members like myself in whispers and well out of earshot. Some claimed to know that she was a drag queen; others pointed to her bust and argued that neither padding nor hormones could produce such a cleavage. Under her flitting

72

but all-embracing gaze we drank till evening, celebrating my prospects, which I indicated were in the field of journalism — there would be an interview, of course, but it would be a walk over. Then back in Earl's Court we made love with something approaching affection.

The address Peter Baillie gave me was that of a basement flat in a square at the back of Harrods. The equivalent of Miss Dalgleish, who had guarded Mr Halcro, was a young woman with an upper-class accent; she wore a silk blouse tied at the neck and secured with a Guards regimental badge in diamonds. She looked at my demob rig-out with some distaste, checked a list on her desk, bade me wait and disappeared into an inner office with a willowy gait. I sat and turned the pages of an old number of *Country Life*, a pile of which lay there as if this were the waiting room of a Harley Street dentist. When she reappeared it was to invite me to go in with an inclination of the head and the suggestion of a smile. The man who sat at the other side of the desk was in his fifties, with a florid face and a large smooth double chin. He wore a discreet club or old boy's tie. 'Weston,' he said in a precise, schoolmasterly voice, holding out his hand which was very soft. He withdrew it hastily. As I sat down he turned the pages of a file with a brown paper cover. 'I see you have a connection with us that goes back to before the war.' He ran his eyes down the page. 'Not a bad war either. Demobbed as major — GSO2 in GSIA BAOR. Excellent references, if I may say so. So I needn't give you a talk about security.' He laughed briefly at his own joke. 'By the way did you handle Ultra?' I saw the trap and said I had no idea what he was talking about. He laughed again and said he was sure I didn't. 'Well,' he went on, 'I believe you have been thinking of journalism. I wonder if I might, as they say, draw a fly over you. It so happens that there are plans to start a journal in which we have a certain interest. It will provide informed and accurate material on the Left in Europe and elsewhere — what goes on in the socialist parties, in the trade unions, who are the important figures, who are the hard-liners, who are the up-and-coming men and where their political loyalties lie, who are the agents and who are merely the naïve tools of the Communists. It is information that might well be of great interest to HMG and to our allies. It will go to the press, to labour correspondents and editors and also to information officers in embassies and consulates. And to representatives of friendly governments. Now I think that if you were to apply for the post of editor — it will naturally have to be advertised — you would stand a very fair chance of landing the job. The salary will be five hundred pounds per annum — not a vast amount admittedly but you will be free to do other things on the side. I needn't spell out the importance and advantage of having someone with your background and experience to run the show. No doubt a lot of useful information will come the way of the editor — whoever he may be,' he gave a slight smile, 'and no doubt he will keep in touch with us. I take it you don't need to be told that there is a national interest that transcends the temporary interests of any government or political party, including the government at present in power. Well, what do you say?'

A curious interview in the St Ermine's Hotel by a board consisting of Weston, a superannuated trade unionist, whom I seemed to remember had held some minor post in the pre-war National Government, and a labour correspondent from *The Times*, got me the job. My formal acceptance landed me in a cramped office on the mezzanine floor of a building in Oxford Street which you entered by a courtyard and a flight of red steps that smelt faintly of urine. It had escaped any real damage during the Blitz but was generally run down. The list of names at the foot of the steps — it included *Socialist International Review* of which I was now the editor — showed the other occupants to be small advertising agencies, property agents and a model agency, which to judge by the young women who went in and out was a cover for a call-girl operation. In three low-ceilinged rooms the *Review* was put together once a month. In the next office to mine sat Bruno Friedenthal, an elderly Austrian socialist with a fierce hatred of Communism. He had come to England in 1936, had never lost his accent nor his habit of dressing in an open-necked shirt and wearing sandals, as if he were about to go hiking with a party of Austrian social-democrats. He was pedantic and naïve, a dreamer of gentle utopias which would emerge more or less painlessly from the womb of time through the inevitable workings of the dialectic. In another age he would have been called 'a fool in God'. Not being connected with 'Mr Halcro' in any way, he carried out with genuine interest and enthusiasm the work of reading long conference reports and detailed, badly typed accounts from his network of correspondents. From them he extracted details of the groupings and re-groupings inside the European labour movement, where he was respected for his courage under repressive regimes in pre-war Austria and laughed at a little behind his back for his child-like candour. In the outer office I had a secretary who, I had been told, was absolutely reliable. Liz was in her mid-thirties, driven by an inward rage at life which had deprived her of her fiancé, shot down over the North Sea in 1942, and now saddled her with an ailing mother with multiple sclerosis in a little flat somewhere in Swiss Cottage. It was her rage that provided the energy with which she typed Friedenthal's prolix accounts of international manoeuvring in the conference halls and committee rooms of the Socialist movement and the precision with which she maintained our confidential card index on personalities on the European Left.

Meanwhile my relationship with Jennifer was relatively stable if somewhat alcoholic. She had contrived to get a job as studio manager in the BBC's Overseas Services in Bush House and worked strange shifts, which had the advantage that we often barely saw each other for days at a time. It was her idea that I should take up Peter Baillie's suggestion and ring Ewan Campbell. When we met it took us only a few minutes, by applying that accurate and well-tried grid familiar to Scots expatriates, to pinpoint our respective origins, educational background and social status. Large, with a beer-belly that protruded through the front of his shirt, Campbell proved to be another son of the manse but of rather grander descent, for his father had been Professor of New Testament Greek at St Andrews University, where Campbell had himself graduated and would also have been ordained had he not gone straight from post-graduate studies at Marburg into broadcasting to Nazi Germany. Over a beery lunch in a pub in the Strand he offered me a voice and language test — largely, I suspected, because I helped to complete a tortuously ingenious *Times* crossword. 'Ah,' he said, as he filled in the last clue, 'you must join the club. I usually reckon to finish it off before the heads of departments meeting at eleven but today I didn't quite manage.' He produced a snuff-box and offered it to me; when I refused he sprinkled the back of his hand, sniffed up the powder and sneezed into a large grubby red and white handkerchief. But my refusal apparently did not disqualify me for a week later I walked for the first time through the immense portico of Bush House, which I found led disappointingly to nowhere in particular except a lot of dingy offices partitioned off with hardboard. In one of them Campbell commissioned me to write a piece on some aspect of the Welfare State. When I handed it in next day he said it wasn't at all bad — just slightly too long. I should remember that eleven English lines was a minute when translated into German. Translated it duly was, and I was coached in the reading of it by an Austrian refugee called Herlitschka, a tall man with a slightly nasal, pinched voice, a long nose and a brown complexion acquired, I imagined, on Hampstead Heath. He treated me with ironical disdain and said he was sure the Soviet and East German monitors would find the talk most interesting. My voice, when I heard it played back after the recording, was strangely different from what it sounded like to me as it vibrated through the bones of my skull and the cavities of my chest. I was not sure that I liked it. The studio manager was a young woman with reddish hair, who shared an elaborate code of jokes with Herlitschka. She was rather tall and would become bony but was quick and intelligent-looking. Herlitschka kissed her hand elaborately as we left with the recording under his arm. I asked Jennifer about her when I got home. She was just stirring after a spell of night-duty and not sociable. But she did admit she recognized my description. 'Sue Godwin,' she said. 'I don't suppose she'll be there long — if you're interested in her. She's put her name down for a transfer to television. Getting in on the ground floor, as they say.'

Soon I was doing pieces for the German Service on a fairly regular basis — on the National Health Service, on trade unionism in Britain, on plans for education, which were slotted into a series called The Changing Face of Britain. Like most people I knew in the Forces I had voted Labour, and with Mr Halcro's blessing from pre-war times was willing to talk about the basis of the Welfare State. I was well informed too, for a mass of material passed through the *Review* office; but I could not help wondering who in Germany listened to me in the cold and hunger of these first post-war years. Perhaps Herlitschka had some grounds for his cynicism but Campbell, returning from one of his visits to what he called his parish, assured us that our voices carried importantly across both the Germanies. East *and* West. He paid and I learned the techniques. Tell them what you are going to say, say it, and tell them you've said it. Cut the first few lines of any talk and give it to the announcer as a lead-in. From the German Service I moved over to the English-language services, broadcasting to the Commonwealth and North America. Once I got a letter from a listener in Tanganyika protesting that a talk by me on the New Towns had glorified a typically Socialist scheme to despoil the countryside, to preserve which had surely been one of Britain's war aims.

ANNOUNCER: Fourteen hours Greenwich Time. You are listening to the General Overseas Service of the BBC. In our series The Changing Face of Britain today's talk is on the New Towns of Britain. The speaker is John Melville.
VOICE: Some fifty miles north of London there is a small town

— or rather a big village. It is like many other places in this rather flat part of central England. There are some rows of what were once the cottages of rural workers. There is a church with a house nearby for the vicar. And of course there is a pub without which no English village would be complete. It is, you might think, if you were to arrive there as I did the other day, a village very much like any other. But it is not. For this village is to be absorbed — swallowed up some people might say — by one of Britain's New Towns.

For England — or rather Britain, since the problem affects all parts of the United Kingdom — has a problem. It is that the old towns and cities have grown too small for the size of the population. This is not merely a result of the immense loss of housing caused by the Blitz. It is due to the fact that since the war the population curve has been rising. There has — perhaps not unexpectedly — been a sharp rise in the number of births since the men who were serving abroad have been reunited with their families. The solution of the problem is a great project to build more or less from scratch a series of new towns. Their planning will be the work of distinguished architects and town-planners. Their streets and roads will be rationally laid out. In the centre will be spacious shopping areas recreating the traditional square which is so common in English country towns. Beyond there will be housing in the English style — flats intermixed with traditional houses with small front gardens and the inevitable lawns. To these houses will come workers and their families who have so far known only the grimy streets of our great towns. And on the periphery will be the factories and warehouses, the railway sidings and depots where they will find employment.

Meanwhile their children will attend the splendid light and airy new schools which are already beginning to spring up. There they will reap the benefits of the Education Act of 1944.

Just outside the village there is a big signboard which says: Welcome to Market Naseborough New Town. The men and women and their families who will move in over the next ten years will find that welcome a warm one.

78

I was beginning to settle down in civvy street, to be accepted in BBC pubs and to make acquaintances in Fleet Street. It was in a pub near the Law Courts that I ran into Brian Napier, his hair thinner than ever and his teeth stained a deeper yellow. He hailed me like a long-lost friend and wondered what I had been up to. I gave him a vague, evasive account of my war and countered with a question about what he had been doing for the last few years. He laughed and said I no doubt knew about that business with the soldiers from the Castle. I feigned ignorance; which led him to explain that he had served a year for incitement to mutiny. I didn't really think, did I, that after that the Army would have him? But he had been in the Auxiliary Fire Service. Did I know about Felicity? I said I did. There was an awkward pause. Then he took himself off with an invitation to look in at his shop in a side-street off the Strand. He had a good selection of secondhand books, pamphlets, paperbacks, folk records — that sort of thing. A good Russian section, too. If I was still interested. As I watched him go with his scarf wound round his neck student-fashion, I remembered the satisfaction with which Mr Halcro had received my gossip about Napier's drinking habits and wondered how far it had gone to decide his fate. I mentioned the meeting when next I saw Weston, having dropped in for a chat about the way things were going at the *Review* and to allay some absurd suspicion, emanating from God only knew where, that Friedenthal, the good sober Friedenthal, was a dangerous Communist. Weston accepted my assurances about Friedenthal but was only mildly interested in Napier about whom they knew already.

During this period I lost sight of Colin. Once I thought I saw him get on to the tube at Earl's Court but the doors shut before I could verify my sighting. Another time I was sure I had glimpsed him entering Brian Napier's bookshop, which was wedged between a depressing café and an establishment with a dingy window full of enemas, curious boxes of pills and discreet advertisements for French letters. A passing bus held me up for a couple of minutes. When I crossed the street and walked in there was no one in the shop except a young man at the cash-desk doodling on a note-pad. The place had a slightly seedy air, as if the proprietor might at any moment emerge to remark confidentially that there was 'stronger stuff in the back, if you fancy it.' I browsed among a stack of old Penguins; the young man was apparently uninterested in me and looked up indifferently when I enquired if Mr Napier was in. He was busy, he replied; no he did not know when he would be free. From behind the door to the bookshop I could hear voices but I could not certainly identify one of them as Colin's and I could not decently linger; so I left. Then one day in 1954 I saw his name on the distribution list of Overseas Talks: Modern English Art by Colin Elphinstone, lecturer in the history of art at the Royal College of Art. It seemed the kind of institution to which he would naturally and effortlessly gravitate. It was not long before we met in the queue in the subterranean canteen at Bush House, full of the din of serving dishes, a polyglot buzz of conversation and the echoing distorted voice that over the tannoy summoned an announcer, a studio manager, a sub-editor back to their duties. As always he greeted me with warmth and surprise, asserting that phoney claim of his that we shared something solid in background and experience. He had still the same soft hair although his face had lost some of its boyish ruddy look. His dress was negligently smart in a way that stood out among the dark suits of the executives, the flannels and pullovers of the exiles. 'Did you know,' he said, 'that it was this sort of place that gave Orwell the idea for *1984*? That's Big Brother on the tannoy!' 'How's Diana?' I asked at a venture. 'Dear Diana — I'm afraid we don't see much of each other these days. Things came unstuck. And you? Still single?' I did not enlighten him about Jenny, who was undecided whether to marry me or to emigrate to Rhodesia where there was sun, no Labour Government, and she had an uncle in the Colonial Service. What had he been doing with himself? At the Courtauld working on a thesis on Austrian Gothic, which meant swanning all over Austria and sampling the wine. Now he was at the

Royal College. Not a bad job but the place was rather stuffy — the senior common room an attempt to achieve a cross between a country house and a gentleman's club. I should come and have lunch one day and see. Meantime there was the canteen lunch to eat, which we did sitting together till joined by Sue Godwin. 'I don't suppose I need introduce you two,' he said. 'Sue's a great girl.' She would do well in television, which was the real place to be now, ghastly as most of it was. I left them with a strong feeling that they were sleeping together. I could tell from the way he lit a cigarette and then handed it to her with a glance that spoke of other more intimate exchanges. I felt a pang of jealousy that was partly sexual, partly professional. As usual it was the ease with which he achieved his ends that riled me. When he felt the time was ripe he too would get a job in television — no doubt he had friends there. Meantime I was stuck with what was beginning to be called 'steam radio', writing talks or taking part in carefully orchestrated discussions on not too ticklish political and social topics. Those of us who took part in these evenhanded discussions were sceptical about the reality of our audience but the fees, though not huge at a guinea a minute, were useful.

One day, going down in the lift to the studios for a discussion on the Budget, I found myself looking at a face which seemed familiar: a curious yellowish complexion and white hair. The man returned my glance without recognition, got out and disappeared along one of the subterranean corridors to the studios.

Sitting at the bar in Grace's where the regular school of liar dice was in session just along the bar, I thought about the face as alcohol gave me its unfailing, familiar shot of warmth and well-being. All afternoon as I sat and drank or gossiped there was an itch at the back of my mind to which I constantly returned, attempting to scratch away the scabs of time that concealed an identity. The puzzle remained with me when I

81

returned to the office to check the messages my secretary had scrawled on my pad with exclamation marks and furious underlinings. I carried it with me along Oxford Street to the tube, then, just as I was about to go underground by the stairway at Oxford Circus, something dispelled the veils of forgetting. I remembered not only where I had seen the face before — in Colin's Hamburg flat — but the name: Hermann Schneider. It was a couple of months before I found an opportunity to speak to him. He was sitting alone in the canteen with a script before him on the table. I quickly bought a coffee and going up to him asked if I might join him. He nodded agreement. I said I believed we had met before — in Hamburg, just after the war — in Colin Elphinstone's flat. Schneider looked at me; his light blue eyes were bright against the curious parchment colour of his face. It was possible, he agreed, but he was afraid he did not remember the occasion. Then taking up his script with the remark that he was on the air in three minutes he gave a slight formal nod and walked off.

I took it for granted that it was Weston who was responsible for the telephone call from a man called Nisbett who said that he would be most grateful if I would look into his office for a moment in the course of the next few days. The address he gave me was familiar, although I had never entered the building, which with its bricked-up ground floor windows and the security desk just inside the curiously blind, secretive entrance, reminded me of some of the headquarters I had worked in during the war. After a confirmatory telephone call to Nisbett's office the man at the desk bade me enter my name in a government-issue ledger before I was led off along anonymous corridors. An open door here and there showed filing cabinets topped by half-empty milk bottles, tin boxes for tea and biscuits, and on the walls fading postcards from last year's holiday resorts. My guide knocked at a door and a voice said 'Come.' Entering, I saw behind a large desk a man in his forties with a bird-like head perched on a remarkable pigeon-chested torso. His eyes were also bird-like, brown and darting. His teeth were large and stained with nicotine. It was impossible to tell, for the desk concealed his extremities, how this strange body continued but since he sat in a wheelchair it was clear that he was in some way crippled. He had asked me to call, he said with a laugh that was birdlike and purely nervous, because he understood I had some experience in the field and, secondly, because he was interested to have my views on a member of the BBC's foreign-language staff who was applying for naturalization. I was no doubt aware that a number of refugees from Germany and Austria had decided they did not wish to return to countries from which they had been absent for fifteen years or more and in which, for obvious reasons, some of them now had neither kith nor kin. Those who had gone back had not always sent encouraging reports. Nor had they always been received with warmth. The years of dictatorship and war had produced changes in the language they had striven to maintain pure in exile. The experiences of political euphoria, of war and defeat had marked the society to which they tried to return in a way that made assimilation difficult. So it was understandable that a considerable number were applying for, and had been granted, British nationality. He apologized for the long preamble but he wanted to put me in the picture. To come to the case in point. One of those who wished to remain — having taken rather a long time to make up his mind — was a certain Dr Herlitschka, an Austrian producer. He would be grateful for my views on him. During this lead-in Nisbett had been meticulously cleaning an ivory cigarette-holder; now he fitted a fresh cigarette into it, and looked at me with his head cocked a little to one side. There were those, he went on, who thought Herlitschka was a bit of a Red but there really was not much on him. In Austria — but that was a long time ago — he had been politically active and had written for various left-wing publications. Since emigrating in 1938 he had been active in the Free German Writers Union and had consistently taken a pro-Soviet line; but in the context of wartime politics that was not unusual. Much could be forgotten and forgiven in that period. He was still some sort of radical but there was no real evidence of political activity. He had some sort of connection with a young woman employed in a secondhand bookshop in Vienna about which our people there had some reservations, but nothing of any weight. Our friend had made a point of looking in there when he was in Vienna on some mission for the BBC but perhaps that could be explained by his penchant for younger women. As I listened I remembered how Herlitschka had bent over to kiss Sue Godwin's hand and how when we met in the subterranean corridors of Bush House or found ourselves together in the queue in the canteen, he would greet me with a tiny, mocking and infinitely condescending bow. I said I knew Herlitschka and had worked with him. The most I could say was that he had indulged in quiet mockery of what went on in Bush House and gave the impression that he found the whole business of broadcasting to Germany rather fatuous. But, to be quite honest, he was not alone in that. His real interest, as far as I could gather, lay in editing the works of a nineteenth century Viennese dramatist called Nestroy. Nisbett said his masters weren't particularly worried about sarcasm. 'There has to be some sort of evidence of political activity of a kind that might be considered detrimental to the society of which the applicant wishes to become a member — otherwise there will be some MP or another getting up to ask awkward questions in the House and my masters don't like that one bit. Nor does the Home Secretary, for that matter,' he gave his birdlike cackle and showed his teeth. 'Not that — between you and me and the gate-post — I have much time for the present incumbent. We were up at Oxford together and I always thought him a bit of an ass.' He paused and picked up a file, opened it and looked at the photograph on the inside of the cover. 'So I think we may say that there is nothing to stand in the way of Dr Alois Herlitschka's becoming a British subject.'

Over time Nisbett and I formed a professional relationship which meant that I passed on to him the sort of material I picked up in the canteen and the bars across the Strand — none of it spectacular, some of it no doubt valuable in contexts of which I was unaware. It was still a surprise when, about a year later, he rang me not about business, as he was quick to explain, but to ask whether I would care to come to dinner. Nothing elaborate because he had to observe a rather strict diet but it would be nice to talk away from 'the fortress'. He wondered if there were anyone I would like to bring with me, but there was no one; Jennifer had left for Rhodesia and I was now a bachelor in the Earl's Court flat, my sexual needs catered for on a commercial basis by a couple of girls in basements down the road. I knew enough about London life by now to surmise that his reasons for inviting me were not entirely social but what other motive he might have was obscure. His address proved to be a ground floor flat in Belsize Park with easy access for a wheelchair through the windows at the back, which gave on to a tiny garden, disconsolate with untrimmed rose bushes going back to briar and rampant creepers. I had been let in by a large bulbous lady dressed in a long velvet sack, who announced in a curiously deep alto voice that she was Dot and vanished into the kitchen. In the room where she left me there was elegant antique furniture. The books on the shelves were polyglot. Above the fireplace hung the deep brown portrait of a gentleman in a wig, with a sharp profile and birdlike eyes. 'Ah,' said Nisbett's voice as he propelled himself in with a powerful thrust on the wheels of his chair, 'my great-great grandfather. He was a Chancery lawyer and apparently a great scoundrel. But we all bear ancestral crosses in our genes. Now this is more pleasing, don't you think?' As he spun across to take a framed pencil drawing from a desk I saw for the first time that he had tiny legs which stuck out straight from the chair and were wrapped in what looked like a thin black tarpaulin. 'This now,' he went on, handing me the drawing, 'is an ancestor of Dot's. Well-known society hostess in the 1890's, friend of Wilde and Whistler, patroness of the arts. It's a Burne-Jones incidentally. Rather fine don't you think? Dot's working on a biography. You can see where she gets her looks and brains from.' As I considered the portrait Dot came in to offer drinks. She bore an unmistakable resemblance to the portrait and might indeed have looked more like it in her youth; but her face had coarsened with the rest of her body. 'Oh, Clive, you're not showing him grandmamma, are you? I'm sure Mr Melville's not the least bit interested.' The sherry was extremely dry and good but they did not linger over drinks. As we moved into the adjoining room Dot asked with great naturalness whether I minded if the children joined us and indicated the two large teddy bears that were already installed at the table. I said of course not. When we had settled in our places Dot leaned over, shook the teddies straight and said severely: 'Now you must sit up very nicely and show Mr Melville how good you can be.' Throughout the dinner, which was unremarkable, for Dot was clearly not interested in cooking and her husband merely picked at a small piece of boiled white fish, they talked to each other through the animals. 'Will you tell Mummy that Mr Melville might like a little more chicken,' to which Dot replied: 'Tell Daddy I was just going to offer him some.' 'I wonder if Mummy would like some more wine?' 'Tell him I mustn't or I shall feel tipsy.' As her voice boomed and his high cackle replied it seemed as if a giant ventriloquist was at work animating them both. It was impossible not to speculate about the mechanisms and nature of their sex-life.

Over the port, while Dot was washing up, Nisbett came to the point, hoping I wouldn't mind talking shop for just a moment.

'It's about a fellow-countryman of yours,' he began, cocking his head in his birdlike way. 'He's been selected for a job as television producer in what the BBC in its wisdom calls Television Talks Department.' He cackled for a moment and wondered what else one could expect from an organization that actually had an executive known as the Director of the Spoken Word. 'Now, of course,' he went on after a pause to savour his joke, 'the candidate has to be "colleged" — another curious term but who am I to quibble at the neologisms of great bureaucracies? — before the appointment is confirmed and I have been asked to do a routine trawl through the files. It is a certain Colin Elphinstone about whom it is thought you might have some knowledge.'

There was an interrogative pause. I waited and wondered whose past was being inspected here: Colin's or mine. Or was that merely a reflex of professional suspicion. Perhaps, he went on — as if to reassure me, he might just rehearse what he himself knew: a good family background — very good, in fact; his father a Writer to the Signet which he took to be something akin to membership of one of the Inns of Court; the son, like his father before him, had had very good war. So he came with the best of references — from, for instance, the erstwhile head of the British Mission to Tito and from an art historian at the Courtauld, where he had been studying — an excellent fellow with whom Nisbett had been up at Oxford and indeed in the same College.

'Now it does seem that at University — both at Oxford and at Edinburgh — but you may know more than I do — Elphinstone got mixed up in some leftish politics, like a lot of other people, of course. I wouldn't like to swear that there isn't the odd Left Book Club volume stuck away in my own shelves.' He made a gesture towards what was presumably his study door. 'Probably collector's pieces by now. Anyway like most people Elphinstone probably got quickly over — what did Lenin call it? — an infantile disorder.' Nisbett cackled briefly. 'I always think that when people like Elphinstone took up politics in the Thirties they were often really playing games. Like the ones they thought up at school. You know the sort of thing. Young men — how shall I put it? — shall we say romantically attached to each other, pretending to be airmen or mountaineers, leaders of one kind or another heading the forces of progress against middle-class philistinism, out-of-date aesthetics, social injustice. And of course, Fascism.'

It was the sort of stuff that got published in the school mag, gave the gutter press a field day, caused bright boys to be sent down and drove parents to distraction. Which gave the players, exhibitionists to a man — and he had known a lot of them —

87

great satisfaction. After all, if one felt inclined to discuss the matter in such terms it was an Oedipal revolt and Franco was everyone's bad Daddy.

'So some of them went off to fight in Spain. Unfortunately politics is for real and — to use that rather nice Americanism — another ball game, with the result that some of them got killed. Rather a waste — don't you think? I expect you remember,' he went on, screwing and unscrewing his cigarette-holder, 'how before the war Eros was regularly boarded up on Boat Race night because the young gentlemen went wild in Piccadilly Circus, knocking off bobbies' helmets and throwing each other into the fountains of Trafalgar Square. Next morning they were up before the beak at Marlborough Street magistrates court where they got a slap on the wrist and a token fine. They were gentlemen kicking over the traces. Which was quite in order. One of the rituals of the tribe.'

He thought — and he apologized for being rather long-winded — that this described Colin Elphinstone very exactly, a young gentleman who had kicked over the traces and probably now wanted to settle down in the BBC. Was his judgement correct? That was the question.

'Well, yes,' I said, 'On the whole I agree. That's where Elphinstone belongs. But I'd go a bit further than you maybe. You see I don't trust romantic and high-minded notions and silly games. Particularly when played by grown-up men. Games can cloud peoples' judgement. Besides the players don't always count the cost. And that can be dangerous.'

'That is a very sober — may I say Presbyterian? — view of things,' said Nisbett contemplating the way the smoke rose from his cigarette, 'but not one to be totally dismissed. Yet our friend seems to have been engaged on some highly delicate operations during the war, which shows that he wasn't exactly seen as a security risk.'

'But mightn't one argue,' I countered, 'that the mission to Tito perhaps required a few political romantics? Apart from being willing to be martyrs in the cause, they'd give the outfit a kind of political acceptability into the bargain. After all

Colin's wireless operator, Tom Pressman — as I know for a fact — was a Communist from away back. And I find it very difficult to believe that the people who set up the Mission didn't know that.' I hesitated for a moment and then decided to play the Ultra joker; if he didn't recognize it there was no harm done. 'So Colin was in the clear, for certain ops, yes, but I'd be astonished if he was ever thought remotely safe enough to be put on the list.'

Nisbett's eyes lit up. 'I take it you were,' he said, lowering his voice conspiratorially. 'I was at Bletchley myself. On the German naval stuff. More exciting than *The Times* crossword, eh? and a lot more difficult.'

So he had recognized the Ultra card; my prestige had obviously increased as a result. I went on to say that I had lost sight of Colin until we met in the Bush House canteen a couple of years ago. To judge by casual conversation, he didn't sound as if he were politically active. If there was no evidence from other sources about politics — subversive politics, that was — (here Nisbett shook his head), I'd be inclined to give him a clean bill of health. With this reservation, that one could never tell with people like Colin when political romanticism, or political sentimentality — whatever one chose to call it — might take over and lead him to make some gesture of disrespect towards the powers that be.

'Well,' said Nisbett, 'we can't legislate for what you will agree is only an interesting hypothesis. Besides, I can't think that in this Talks Department he is going to have a great deal to do with sensitive — I love these official euphemisms, don't you? — areas or sensitive topics. As I understand it he will be concerned chiefly with the arts. So a clean bill of health it is even if he does seem to have a *faible* for the fair sex. But at least he's not a queer. Mark my words, queers are nearly all security risks. That was most helpful. I'll have a word with the BBC Appointments Officer tomorrow.' On cue Dot, who had been discreetly busying herself in the kitchen arrived with the coffee, and we turned to other things such as my Scottish background on which they examined me like a couple of anthropologists faced by a member of some remote and fascinating tribe.

My way home that night took me back across the Heath to the address in a better part of Hampstead, where I had lived now for a couple of years in a single-storied brick building: an outhouse? a Victorian *dépendance* built for whom? an old nanny? an indigent maiden aunt? an alcoholic brother? At all events set at a safe distance at the far end of a large tangled garden that belonged to a fine house. Built in the year of Waterloo, my landlady had said, as she showed me what the advertisement had described as 'a studio with a kitchen and bathroom en suite'. It was, in fact, one long room with a balcony; off it was a tiny cooking-space and beyond that a loo and a shower. She had been quick to point out that it had a private entrance in the lane at the end of the house — a facility, she hinted, I might appreciate as a single gentleman. She herself was divorced, living comfortably enough in the great house with its original heavy wooden shutters and paved floors, and did not wish to lose her generous alimony by remarrying. But over the months after I moved in we had formed a relationship based on visits from her to me or, less frequently, from me to her: unsentimental occasions which she determined. Her code-word for them was 'drinkies'. She would announce her coming by a note slipped under the door giving on to the garden from my studio or by a brief and business-like phone-call. Sometimes we would indeed only drink by the heat of the tall copper stove that in winter burned night and day in my studio; on other occasions we would move to the mattress on the balcony, displacing a large ginger tom called Mr Halcro, who took himself off unwillingly. Before yielding she had to have had enough liquor to blame her acquiesence on its effects; but if I uttered some conventional expression of affection she was liable to push me away with: 'You only say that so I won't put up the rent.' Tonight there was no note and no call on my answering-machine. Looking across the lawn where the brown daffodils, carefully knotted, marked the outlines of a little cemetery for generations of

Victorian pets, I could see the light in her bedroom where she no doubt lay in her shortie nightdress reading romantic novels. For she was given to a romantic view of life, so that a call that proved to be a wrong number was her husband checking up on her, someone planning a break-in — 'So you'd better spend the night, but no sex, mind!' — or her daughter, safely married to a New Zealand businessman given to birdwatching, cricket- and rugby-matches, announcing some domestic tragedy. The fact that I had been in intelligence she found 'exciting' but she expected I couldn't talk about it. She thought of intelligence in terms of spy-catching and cloak-and-dagger work; she had no conception of that side of war which deals in card-indexes.

The diaries are lined up in the top drawer of the filing cabinet beside my desk which is at the far end of the studio from the balcony. Mr Halcro likes to lie on top in an old copper preserving pan, one paw dangling limply over the edge. All the years since the war. Names — telephone numbers — times of planes and trains — notes of expenses — deadlines. The date when Jennifer left for Rhodesia. The date when I met H. The coded + that marks our love-making.

On 1 March 1960 (St David's Day) H. came to see me to talk about the Histraduth and Israeli labour politics. She worked for the Foreign Affairs committee of the Labour Party. Her name actually was Helen Gordon. She was the wife of a Labour MP for a Midland constituency with a safe majority, a lawyer by profession. We got on well together. Met again. Had meals together. Talked. Were drawn to each other. In what I recognized as an attempt to draw back she invited me to a disastrous dinner-party at her place where I felt embarrassed, gauche and became rather drunk and argumentative. I thought that would be the end of it but we made up and continued to meet and to move, drawn by liking, desire, hopes that were perhaps impossible, fantasies of which we were reluctantly, intermittently conscious, towards that transitory moment when our linked bodies would promise permanence, union, joy everlasting.

She was (is) not beautiful but lively and very funny. Intelligent. Warm. My secretary, Liz, hated her. 'That woman,' she would say as she put through her calls.

The first time we made love it was on the floor of the office. We had been to see an Italian film at the Academy Cinema just down Oxford Street. A very funny film about a gang of housebreakers. We laughed a lot. Afterwards we had a meal at an Italian restaurant which has since vanished.

She said once that what she couldn't stand in her marriage were the pressures. The visits to and from his parents and her parents. The woman who called just before the wedding and left literature on how a good Jewish wife should behave, about her uncleanness, which did not end so long as there was a spot of blood the size of a shilling. Her mother constantly asking when she could look forward to being a grandmother. Her husband, ambitious, busy in the House, on committees, at surgeries in his constituency, addressing meetings, looking to be noticed by the big men on the front bench. Practically making a date to sleep with her. His connivance with her mother, so that when he found out they confronted her together. The mother saying she was behaving like a cat on heat. And not even with 'one of our people'. Charles — 'like a son to me he is' — asking sullenly whether he had ever denied her anything. Had he not given her a good house and allowed her every freedom, like having a job? Travelling alone. And what had she done with that freedom? The shame would kill her father, that was her mother's theme. There would be a divorce. A scandal. Headlines in *The News of the World*. MP's Wife in Divorce Scandal. Not to mention *The Jewish Chronicle*. She would not be able to put her face outside the house. Thank God she didn't have long to live. But her poor father. Another stroke would finish him off.

She held out for weeks. Then she broke. She came to my

office one evening in December, late, when I was alone. She wept. I wept. She said she was pregnant. Whose was it? She didn't know. We made love with a kind of desperation.

I think she was being absolutely truthful when she said she didn't know whose child it was.

Just before Christmas, that December of 1960, I almost ran into her on Westminster Bridge. I had been to the House to talk to some MP or other. She saw me coming and, turning back, ran down into the underground.

We spent two nights together in all — at an International Socialist Conference in Rome. The hotel, I remember, was called the *Albergo d'Inghilterra*. Near the Spanish Steps.

The Manchester Guardian 23 August 1961: Gordon — To Tony and Helen (née Marcus) at Hampstead General Hospital, a son, Joel.

In the days and months following the break with Helen I was often absent from the office. Especially in the afternoon. I was, after all, a machine, safe in the industrious hands of Friedenthal, who each month faithfully put together long accounts bristling with acronyms: PSDI, PSI, CSIL, CGI, SPD, KPD. In the pages of the review what were presumably the passionate aspirations of large numbers of men and women were reduced to grey prose. I had seen the back numbers stacked dustily in the offices of press and labour attachés in embassies at home and abroad. Of course, there was the confidential card-index to be kept up-to-date, but Liz was perfectly capable of doing that from the notes I passed to her: information gleaned from conferences — like that one in Rome which I remembered sadly, recalling a glow of sex and happiness — or from talks with a man attached to the American Embassy who gave out that he was a member of the American Socialist, which was perhaps a professional joke. Even Friedenthal, who had a sure judgement in such matters, said he was probably a CIA operative. At all events he was an invaluable source of information on the European parties of the Left, their tendencies and the degree to which they had been infiltrated by the Communists. Occasionally there would be a query from Weston but they were rarely urgent and Liz could stall till next day when I arrived, somewhat hungover, to deal with them. The reasons for the enquiries were usually as obscure to me as those about the names on my German order of battle in Cairo. But once, attending out of curiosity an extradition hearing involving a German student believed by the authorities to be a political danger (Friedenthal maintained they had got things wrong), I heard counsel for the Home Office conjure with names I recognized from my collection. But that was no reason why I should not take off after lunch and spend my afternoons in warmth that was partly the fug of the basement that housed Grace and her realm, partly the slow seepage of the alcohol through my system. From Grace's I would return, often after both Friedenthal and Liz had gone, and read the furiously underlined list of messages, reminders and threats on my desk. At first I made excuses, inventing alibis — a recording session at Bush house, a meeting with a German socialist deputy passing through London — but Liz quickly unmasked me. She threatened to resign then thought better of it, for the job was safe, the pay reasonable, and her boss not fussy — what right had I to be? — about how long she took shopping for her invalid mother or about her time-keeping. So I became a regular, a truant in the cave where Grace, whatever her gender, dispensed anaesthetizing liquor.

It was far into one afternoon at Grace's that I decided to phone Colin. To be precise it was in the second week of January 1961, a couple of weeks after H. had escaped me down the subway. Grace was sitting as usual enthroned just by the cash register, behind her an array of postcards, coloured, gaudy, scribbled with messages in which sexual insinuations were mixed with parodies of commonplace greetings: Bangkok. Having a lovely time, dear, banging away. On a shelf above her head were miniature dolls in folk costume from the airport shops of all five continents and (her most prized possession) certain beautiful pieces of glass which she claimed were antique dildoes. As usual she was talking in a regal way with favoured customers, turning every now and then to adjust in the mirror behind the bar a ringlet of her complicated, towering coiffure or to examine a tiny flaw in her nails. Meanwhile the work of serving fell on Malcolm, a Scots boy with delicate features and darkening but natural blonde hair, which he tossed back from his eyes with a swift and graceful movement of the head, as he poured the gins, double whiskys and brandies with Grace's eye constantly flicking towards him to check the accuracy of his measures. He was, I guessed from his accent, a working-class boy from Dundee or Fife, who had found in the club a spot where he could freely display his ambivalent sexuality. Both Grace and Malcolm watched speculatively as I made my way to the phone which was in a narrow corridor leading to the gents. The wall was covered with names, telephone numbers and a higher class of graffiti: references to falls from Grace, Grace abounding and Grace before and after meat, which she not only tolerated but referred to pointedly, claiming to know the author of each one. The secretary in Colin's office was dubious and defensive. Perhaps she was new. She asked me to repeat my name. There was a long pause — a dead interval during which I could envisage her holding her hand over the mouthpiece as she spoke to someone: Colin? When she came back on the line it was to say: 'He seems to have gone out for a moment. Can I help you?' It was about my unhappiness, I could have said. About the way alcohol could only partially lull the pain lying there within my breast at that point where 'I' existed; that there was, I felt, with however little justification some sort of link between us that went back a long way because chance had thrown us together many times; that he was at the same time sufficiently remote for me to speak to him without shyness and yet close enough to make me feel safe in speaking. I said none of this, merely that he was an old friend of mine, that I had rung to try to arrange a meal — it was purely personal. She listened coolly. I believed I

95

could hear the rustle of paper as she moved things about on her desk or opened some incoming mail. She would let Colin know, she said. The next time I rang he was away filming. Abroad. No, she did not know exactly when he would be back. The third time he was, she said at a meeting. Did he have my number? She would ask him to ring me back. He never rang. There were, I knew, various possibilities: that she was merely being a good watchdog; that she had decided that this voice, slightly thick from the whisky, belonged to someone Colin need not bother with; or that she had signalled Colin and got a No. When I discussed it with Sue Godwin — much later when we were briefly 'together', if that word can describe an intimacy so fraught with distance — she merely said: 'Well, why should he want to talk to you?' I had been an idiot, I had no real connection with Colin (had anyone?) and Colin was no man's comforter. But I experienced it as a betrayal I resented and could not forgive.

Sue and I got together after a party given by her boss, whose list contained a number of modish radical authors but who in his own office stamped out trade unionism with a mixture of blackmail, bribery and the sack. The party was for a dissident author from Hungary, in honour of whom a good deal of Bull's Blood was drunk with the result that in the course of the evening Sue got rather tight and allowed me to take her home to her flat, where I found myself accepted as another member of the household along with Penelope, her stay-at-home dog. What we might, had we formulated the thought, have described as mutual comfort was in fact the attempt to anaesthetize by sex our separate miseries. If I still mourned H., Sue had had a nervous breakdown — a case of sheer exhaustion, physical and moral — brought on by her role in Colin's life and career and its sudden termination. It was as if she had been sucked dry by him. She never spoke of their relationship and I did not ask. From the inevitable small remarks, asides, hints, glancing references she let fall, it sounded as if it had developed from being a short and tumultuous affair into a close but essentially professional relationship, with sex perhaps occasionally thrown in on foreign assignments or when they worked long on some project in his flat above Regent's Park. Nor did I ever speak of H. She did though when she was angry, accusing me of still being in love with her and maintaining that given half a chance I'd go back to her tomorrow: which was true. So in our own ways we sustained each other with sex and whisky. Then one day out of the blue she asked for her key back and gave me till six o'clock to move out. But we still saw each other, still drank together, watched the telly together, exchanged gossip. I neither knew — nor cared — who shared the little bedroom (nor how often) at the back of the flat where we had lain and heard the early morning goods trains go clanking by. If we were still linked, it was by our unspoken common relationship to Colin and by our work for our respective 'Mr Halcro's', which took her into the world of exiles and dissidents whose book she edited and whose needs she catered for — not usually personally, although it did happen — but by recruiting trust-worthy people like myself as minders to amuse them, drink with them, help them to get women, take them to the stripjoints of Soho. But to Grace's I would not take them; that was increasingly my haven and refuge.

Among the regulars at Grace's was Bill Gilchrist, a professional Scotsman, who exchanged banter with Malcolm, the barman, in a broad accent and laced his conversation for the benefit of Sassenachs and other outsiders with patter on the lines of 'it's a braw, bricht munelicht nicht the nicht.' Crime reporter on a Sunday paper, he claimed to be in the confidence both of the police and of the barons of the underworld in their manors down the Old Kent Road. He had photographs of himself along with various hard cases and equally hard-looking blondes. He also hinted at links with Special Branch and the security services. His background was obscure and he deliberately kept it so. Not even in the course of long and slightly maudlin conversations about Scotland could I positively discover where he haled from, or what his origins were. From time to time he would disappear, returning to recount how he had been doing 'a wee bit fishing' — for salmon naturally — with friends in the Highlands or having a few days on the moors with the guns. His accounts lacked essential precision. Once I caught him out in his geography of the trout streams of my own county but he fudged his mistake with not more than a second's hesitation. His dress was vaguely rural. His hats lacked only a trout or salmon fly in the hat-band. His highly polished shoes were a townsman's version of brogues; his suits were fine, well-cut tweeds. A green and brown Paisley handkerchief spilled from his breast pocket. When he shot his cuffs — a gesture so frequent as to be almost a tic — he revealed gold cuff-links set with a large green stone. He carried his cigarettes in a slim silver case; his lighter, which he wielded with a flourish, was elaborately initialled. His was a fox's face, long and pointed, with brown eyes and reddish hair; the skin was mottled with curious white patches as if he had been burned or suffered from some kind of disease. His talk was very grand, whether it concerned the Home Office official with whom he had dined the night before, the senior policeman who had invited him to a boxing match, or the starlet he had squired to some house-party in a villa on the Thames. Where he lived was a mystery. Malcolm claimed to know that he had a flat in Shepherd's Market off Piccadilly, a suitably louche neighbourhood with red lights in the doorways where young models invited visitors and on the pavements the older whores solicited custom. He claimed to know, too, that Bill had started as a message-boy on the Dundee *Courier and Advertiser*, his parents being decent bodies who used to have a baker's shop in the Bowgate.

Gilchrist had picked up from odd references that I had an Intelligence background and tried to sound me out about Ultra. What, he wanted to know, had really gone at that place north of London, Bletchley, where a lot of weirdos had been working on some very funny high-level stuff. When I denied all knowledge he laughed and called me 'a downy bird'. These were the post-Burgess and Maclean days, when the traffic in stories of defectors flourished and there were theories about what Gilchrist called 'pinkos' in the institutions of the Establishment. If he felt like it, he indicated, he could name a few — and would do so when the time was ripe — in the Civil Service, in the BBC, in the trades unions (of course) and even in the Church of England. When discussing such matters he hinted at sources high in the security services and claimed to be able to name the unmentionable head of MI5. Perhaps it was a tactic to conceal the extent of his true knowledge that such claims were mixed with others so extravagant that even I, who had some inkling of these matters, was lost in a magma of truth and fantasy. But I was not altogether surprised — for he was capable of great accuracy — when he brought up the name Schneider.

I already knew about the Schneider affair from Nisbett. Since my calculated indiscretion about being 'on the list' he had treated me to certain professional confidences. He rang me up one day, wondering if I might look in some time so that he could pick my brains about something that had come up. That something proved to be a situation in the BBC's German Service. 'You may know from your own contacts,' he began, screwing a cigarette into his holder, 'that the text of a talk to the so-called German Democratic Republic has been leaked to a left-wing journal, which has reproduced it. The journal in question has a tiny readership on the wilder fringes of the Left but it is just the sort of thing that some journalist might pick up. Not that there was anything startling in the talk, which merely reflected H.M. Government's view on Berlin — but it's the kind of rabbit that, once it's out of the bag, a whole pack will be after.' He examined the ash at the end of his cigarette before sticking the holder back in his mouth and continuing, squinting at me through the smoke. 'But the leak is one thing. What is more serious is that there seem to have been several occasions when the texts of talks have been changed during transmission.' He didn't need to tell me that there was what — on the face of it — looked like an effective system of editorial control. The translators of the main political commentaries, normally written in English by British-born members of staff — or outside British-born contributors, like myself — were thoroughly reliable. That left only the German readers. One of them had been making alterations in the scripts — nothing obvious, rather a question of nuances, the blunting of a point, the use of a particular word. The overall result had been to make texts more acceptable to the ears of those Eastern bureaucrats who in due course read the monitoring reports, and in so doing to give a false impression, for instance, of HMG's determination to uphold the status of Berlin in the face of the Soviet threats and attempts to destabilize — to use another new coinage — the situation there. It had to be said that the BBC had been rather slow in tumbling to what had been going on. Perhaps they had forgotten that the rigorous checking of output at the point of transmission which had been normal in wartime was also necessary in conditions of Cold War. But they had wakened at last, started recording off transmission and had caught Mr Hermann Schneider in *flagrante delicto*. But not before he had somehow got the text of the talk on Berlin out of the building and passed it on to the publisher of this wretched, almost unreadable rag. We didn't need to worry too much about Mr Schneider, who was only on short-term contract and was already out on his ear and no doubt out of the country. What was more important was the background to the whole affair. How did Schneider get taken on in the first place? Did no one have any idea that he was — let us say — politically suspect? Who were his contacts on the Left? How did he manage to convey the text to the curious socialist or communist monthly? Now what might or might not be significant was that Schneider had been taken on on the warm recommendation of our friend — odd, wasn't it, how

100

his name kept cropping up? — Colin Elphinstone. Elphinstone had of course been seen. And he had been perfectly open about the whole business. Yes, he had recommended Schneider to Ewan Campbell. He had known Schnieder at the radio station in Hamburg at the end of the war. Schneider had written to him out of the blue saying he would welcome the opportunity to come to England to improve his English and do some broadcasting to support himself meantime. So he had put in a word for him on the basis of his high opinion of Schneider's talents as a broadcaster. Yes, he had known that Schneider was of the Left but so far as he, Elphinstone, knew he did not belong to any proscribed organization and was in any case more interested in writing — he was a considerable poet — that in politics as such. His poetry did have a political edge but not a party-political one. He had seen very little of Schneider since his arrival in Britain, having himself been abroad a good deal on assignments connected with his programme. He regretted he could not cast more light on the affair. Nisbett laid down the file from which he had been reading. 'Unless our friend is a consummate liar he seems to be in the clear. What do you think?'

'What one doesn't know,' I said, 'is just how sentimental Elphinstone is.' At the word 'sentimental' Nisbett looked quizzically at me and blew a cloud of smoke. 'Sentimentality,' I went on, 'in the sense of romantic attachment to the feelings and emotions — and ideas of the past. Specifically to the ideas of the Left of the thirties. Some people's development is arrested in the sense that they are still stuck in the War — you know the kind, clinging to wartime ranks and wartime slang — others are stuck in the politics of pre-war years.' 'Which you would describe in Elphinstone's case, I take it, as a matter of the heart rather than of the mind,' said Nisbett. He considered for a second or two. 'And that means?' 'That his judgement of Schneider might be clouded.' 'All right — but it's not much to go on. I wonder — you couldn't possibly talk to Elphinstone, about Schneider, I mean? Quite informally, of course,' I ignored the suggestion. 'There is, of course,

101

another possibility.' 'Which is?' 'That he is covering up for Schneider.' And I told him of my sighting of Colin entering Napier's bookshop. 'Well, it's always something,' said Nisbett, clearly somewhat surprised. 'Not much though — not much of a — what do the boys in blue call it?' 'A lead,' I suggested. 'That's right, a lead.'

I did ring Colin, at his office. This time I got through. We exchanged the usual trivialities about work and how life was treating us. Then:

'Listen, Colin — you know about the row over Schneider?'

'Know? I was grilled for ages.'

'I'd like to talk to you about Schneider some time.'

'I really haven't an awful lot to say. I'm pretty busy just now — getting a new programme series together. Why don't you call again in a month's time. We can have a drink or something. Or better still — why don't I call you when I get back from location? I must have your number somewhere.'

Naturally he did not call.

I think it was from this time that there began what Sue was to call the hunting of the Snark.

When next I saw Weston I brought up the subject of Napier and Schneider. He was dismissive. Napier was — or put it about that he was — disillusioned with Stalin's brand of Communism. Probably a Trotskyist subscribing — as I no doubt knew — to a heady political theory based on a romantic view of history that looked back to a revolutionary golden age and forward to an apocalyptic future. But it might of course be quite simply a cover-up for a position and an allegiance that had not basically changed. Schneider had gone back to East Germany and was now a regular broadcaster there. I should get Nisbett to let me see the reports from the BBC's Monitoring Service. All very predictable stuff. He made a motion with his hand towards his in-trays as if to indicate that he now had other things to do than talk about such matters; but I lingered and said that what interested me was the link between Napier and Schneider. 'Oh, yes,' said Weston, 'and what might that be?' 'Colin Elphinstone.' 'You really think so?' he asked incredulously. 'There's nothing on him — nothing of any importance. Some peccadilloes from the thirties. But there are people on the Labour front bench who were active in the Young Communist League in those days. We don't necessarily hold it against them. But if you can come up with anything solid of course I should be interested.'

'I wonder why I did it?'

'Did what?'

We had been watching Colin interview a rising young actress in a miniskirt so short as to cause Sue to wonder whether everyone was going to be walking around looking like something out of *As You Like It*.

'Give him a clean bill of health.'

As Colin turned away from the actress with a gesture of thanks that was more, I suspected, than a mere public formality, and brushing the hair from his brow, announced the name of the celebrity he would interview next week, I switched off the set.

'Damn it,' said Sue, 'I wanted to see the end titles.'

'Still living in the past,' I said. 'Assistant to the producer: Sue Godwin.'

She made no reply but poured herself another whisky, laughed and said: 'Why you did it? I think I know why'. She paused as Penelope woke and came across to lay her head on her knees. 'First of all, he's rotten with charm, our Colin. It comes right out of the screen. Which is why all the maiden ladies in Cheltenham send him fan-mail, knit him gloves — for filming in winter, don't you know — and love everything about him from the limp he manages so beautifully to that boyish smile. The sudden seriousness. The way he puts his hair back from his forehead. He's irresistible, I tell you.'

'You should know.'

'Never mind me. It's you we're talking about. Shall I tell you something? You have always fallen for his charm. Don't you remember how you used to join us in the canteen and let it wash over you? Then there's the Scottish bit, which I confess I don't understand. But it's there. You say you hate the place — never want to go back. All that. But put you and Colin together and at the drop of a hat you start trotting out the odd dialect word and telling unfunny stories. The only other lot that go on like you Scotsmen are the Jews. It's got something to do with belonging to a tribe. As you should know.'

I said nothing.

'I'll tell you something else. It's not just that you are envious of him. It's not ordinary jealousy — just because he's on the telly and you're stuck with steam radio and the boring old *Socialist Review*. Somewhere, dear boy, as our Colin would say, you're in love with him. I don't suppose for a moment he'd ever notice. He doesn't notice when people are in love with him. Too wrapped up in himself. Too busy being Colin.'

It was Gilchrist who brought up the name of Schneider. Approaching me in the bar at Grace's, 'Jock,' he said, although he knew I disliked this appellation, shooting his cuffs before extracting a cigarette and tapping it methodically on his silver cigarette case, 'Jock, you do the odd bit of work for the BBC in Bush House. A wee bird tells me there's been a bit of a stramash there recently — in the German Service to be precise. I'm told a member of the staff got the push. A Red of some kind who's gone back to where he belongs — to East Germany. You wouldn't have picked up anything in the canteen now, would you? I hear it's a great place for gossip. Malcolm, Mr Melville's glass needs refreshing. Straight malt? It's the only drink. I canna stand that blended stuff either.'

Yes, I agreed, there had been some trouble. Did I know any names? Schneider, a short-term import from Germany. Did I happen to know anything about this fellow Schneider's past? As a matter of fact I did, I said, feeling the comforting warmth of the liquor. But anything I said was naturally not for attribution. I had met Schneider in Hamburg just after the war, working for Hamburg radio and in some difficulty because of his politics. 'John man,' said Gilchrist, 'I always kent ye had a lot of interesting things tucked away in that head of yours. But very tight you are, very secure.' How had I come to know this Mr Schneider? I emptied my glass and reflected. Then I heard myself, rather far off as it seemed, say: 'I met him through Colin Elphinstone.' Gilchrist slapped his hand on the top of the bar so that the ash flew off his cigarette and settled in flakes on his suit. Grace looked up disapprovingly from a conversation about the relative merits of Mallorca and Benidorm as places to withdraw to in one's old age — not that Grace had any intention of retiring yet. By no means. 'I knew it,' said Gilchrist, 'I knew it, I can smell them a mile off. I've sat at home watching that smoothie talk about art. Licking the arses of so-called painters and writers, cracking up stuff any school-kid could do with one hand. You can always spot them — at least I can. I tell you they're right in there — plugging their fancy ideas about art and shouting blue murder about censorship and rights for queers. What they're after is to poison the mind of the viewers — to break things up. Because that's what they want — to destroy everything that's decent in our society. But I'll fix him, you'll see. And the Beeb as well.'

The Sunday Record: 19 October 1964

THE RED ANNOUNCER

Has the BBC been penetrated by agents from the East?
A Special Report by Bill Gilchrist

A man who may well have been an agent for the so-called

German Democratic Republic has succeeded in penetrating the Overseas Services of the BBC. These Services, may I remind our readers, are maintained at the expense of the taxpayer.

The man, whose name is being kept under wraps for security reasons, was employed to broadcast for the German Service. He was caught red-handed fiddling the texts he was employed to read — texts which told the brave men and women who listen to the Voice of London the truth about the Cold War.

I understand that the man in question has already left the country. Indeed you can hear his voice on the East German radio broadcasting ridiculous lies about this country.

It now remains to discover who was responsible in the first place for this gaffe. I understand that there has been an internal inquiry. But how thorough was that inquiry? Did it, for instance, look into the connections between the agent and a certain BBC employee, now working for television, who has a known record of left-wing sympathies?

As readers of this column know, there has been an uneasy feeling in some quarters that the BBC has an assortment of Pinkos on its payroll and has done very little to root them out.

I understand the matter is likely to be raised in the House. It will be interesting to see what answer the mandarins of Broadcasting House come up with.

In a written reply to A. Gordon, Derby N, the Postmaster General stated that he understood from the BBC that there had been a full internal enquiry into the leakage of the text of a broadcast in the German language to the press and that the matter was now closed.

I watched my landlady's light go out and climbed up to my mattress in the balcony. As I settled down Mr Halcro explored me, his breath fetid with cat-food, before curling himself to settle on the duvet at my back. Lying there with the warmth of the beast seeping through to me, I reflected on my betrayal and explored that focus of jealousy which had inspired it: the grudge that rankled because of his ease in the world, that silver-spooned advantage which had led him to fame — well, not to fame, to prominence — while I must count myself fortunate to be bored at the *Review*. But it was his freedom I chiefly envied. It was as if he feared no authority (but then he could afford not to do so) while I kissed the rod, heeded the powerful and brought my little bits of information to the 'Mr Halcro's' of this world, those powerful secretive men who because he was of their class, pardoned as peccadilloes actions which in others would have been black marks on their files, barring them without explanation from promotion or employment, placing them under suspicion for years. Meanwhile there was Colin on the box week after week, charming, knowledgeable, appearing on film among the ruins of some ancient civilization, discussing without pedantry the work of some painter, poet or architect. For whatever internal enquiry had been carried out it manifestly had not affected Colin's status and reputation. Indeed the rumour was that he now felt so secure professionally that he intended to go freelance, become an independent producer and sell his programmes himself on the market. I lay there sleepless, so that Mr Halcro, disturbed by my tossing, rose indignantly and took himself off to a place downstairs beside the stove. I revolved my suspicion of that political sentimentality which was liable to colour the actions of men and women long after any clear, overt political commitment had been abandoned; which was Colin's case, as I had to admit. For in spite of attempts to recruit him by young men and women, younger than himself, whose attentions were no doubt flattering, he steered a careful course through the radicalism that surrounded him in the world where he now moved. If he put his signature to an appeal, appeared on a platform, he clearly weighed his actions carefully and spoke unexceptionably in terms of artistic freedom, freedom of thought and speech and against censorship in literature and the arts. What then were the grounds for my suspicion? Sue was clear. I was neurotically involved with this man who rode

107

so easily on the winds of fortune and who was still 'as fresh as is the month of May' — perhaps a little marked now by time, not yet autumnal but just passing his high-summer mark and about to decline into handsome age. This man who, when we met, claimed close acquaintance on which one could not rely, for it too was part of the role he played.

Notes on paranoia:
Paranoia: *Path*. Mental derangement: spec. chronic mental unsoundness characterized by delusions and hallucinations. Hence Paranoiac a. afflicted by paranoia (OED)
In paranoia the projection of a reproach on another person without any consideration for reality becomes manifest as the process of forming delusion. (Freud?)
Paranoia: Chronic psychosis characterized by more or less systematic delusion. Freud places erotomania, delusional jealousy and delusions of grandeur under the heading of paranoia. It should be noted that paranoia is defined in psychoanalysis, whatever the variation in the delusional mode, as a defence against homosexuality. (Some book Sue was editing once.)

At the publisher's party there was the usual collection of Sovietologists, academic groupies and sad exiles. I balanced a glass of acidulous wine and gulped a moist sandwich filled with some bland white subtance. A little Hungarian with jowls like a basset hound was explaining to me that Africans were by nature backward. He knew because he had taught mathematics in a West African University, a post he had admittedly accepted solely to be able to defect to the West. 'Just out of the trees, I think you say,' he went on. Of course it was not nice to talk about the question of race and people avoided it, especially at cocktail parties where one never knew who might be listening, but the question was there and would not go away. Take Russia: its ultimate tragedy was not Bolshevism, which would collapse from internal stresses, but the fact that in the course of the twenty-first century, Russia, in which I should remember he had grown up, would be the victim of mongolization as the peoples of the Asian republics proliferated and the birth-rate of European Russia fell. This led him on to Vietnam and the need to avoid squeamishness, which was something that unfortunately tended to affect Western statesmen. There had been no real problem about dropping the bomb on Hiroshima and Nagasaki — acts which history had fully justified — so why did the United States not simply drop one on Hanoi? Why should all these American soldiers die just to salve the conscience of the West? He looked up into my face. 'I expect I shock you, Mr Melville. You liberals are so naïve. You will never learn — or only when it is too late.' There was a pause during which he balanced on his heels and looked carefully round the room. 'I know all the CIA people here,' he said at length, 'but I wonder who the KGB agents are. Because you know, my innocent friend, there are bound to be some here. They would not wish to miss such an occasion.' He laughed. 'I see your charming friend, Miss Godwin. She can look very handsome, don't you think? With the honoured guest, Mr Semyonov. But she's not his type. If I know anything about that drunken Russian peasant — who is of course very gifted — it is that he likes them large and very white-skinned.' He was off down the room with his rolling gait, bowing slightly to Sue as he passed. With Semyonov in her wake she made towards me. He had straw-coloured hair and a pale, pointed face: a peasant boy turned intellectual and poet. I could not help thinking of Esenin, that other peasant-poet, who drank himself to death. Semyonov looked as if he might be taking the same road. His eyes were a little glazed; as he approached he grabbed a glass from a passing waitress with a deft motion. Sue presented me as a journalist and broadcaster, who would be happy to show Mr Semyonov more of London: she was sure — she added with a touch of irony — that we would find many interests in common. Semyonov was neither impressed nor interested. He swayed slightly and gazed past me. His eyes rested on a lecturer from

109

the School of Slavonic studies: a pale-skinned, plump New York Jewess with rather fat legs and large breasts. Semyonov watched her intently and then said in heavily accented but accurate English: 'I have not had a Jewess. Will you please introduce me.' Sue managed to catch the eye of his prey and signalled to her to come over. She disengaged herself and moved placidly towards us with her wide smile and brown eyes. The introductions over, she and Semyonov moved off speaking Russian. When next I saw them they were in a corner by the bar. Semyonov was stroking her bottom and staring at her breasts. I passed Sue in the throng and nodded in their direction. She followed my glance and shrugged. 'In the book we are publishing,' she said, 'by the way have you got a review copy? — they're over there on the table — he says life would be much easier if one were a eunuch. I expect you'd agree.' I ignored her sarcasm and said he didn't look like one to go in for self-mutilation. When in due course the security people found him dead in the Streatham flat where they had installed him, he had not only cut his own throat but had first hacked off his penis.

'There's Colin,' Sue said suddenly, 'I wondered if he would actually turn up.' She moved off to where he had just made an entrance, pausing for a moment at the door, looking round from under his thickening eyebrows and then moving with that almost imperceptible Byronic limp of his towards the drinks. The limp was something that came and went according to what he was feeling like and to the situation; thus it was more pronounced when he was tired or when, as now, he merely wished to be remarked. No war wound, it was the result of a crash in which he overturned a car on the way back from an officers' club in the British Zone of Germany. He had been a little tipsy and was lucky to get away with a damaged leg. His companion, a young woman from the Control Commission, was less lucky; she smashed her face against the windscreen. Our host the publisher, Sue's boss, made quickly towards him. Semyonov, who was by now far gone in drink, was detached from his prey long enough to meet the man

110

from television, presenter of a distinguished programme on literature and the arts, who would no doubt be interested to interview Mr Semyonov about his new book: *Flowers of Ice*. Semyonov was immensely pale and haughty. He feigned not to understand English and summoned his new friend to interpret for him. He would, he let it be known through her American college-girl voice, be most honoured to be interviewed by Mr — . His interpreter could not easily conceal the ironical tone of his reply. Colin said he would like to consider the idea and would be in touch with Mr Semyonov through his publisher, then, looking over the heads of the crowd, sought refuge. He found it in me. I had not met him since Gilchrist's intervention in the Schneider affair; but that was now old history from which Colin had emerged apparently unscathed. 'What are you doing in this *galère?*' he asked but did not wait for an explanation. 'My God,' he went on, 'Stalin was responsible for a lot, wasn't he? What's the book like? Is there an item for the programme there? Not too long. Is it true he doesn't speak English?' I said I thought Semyonov would be all right when sober but that, for the moment, his thoughts and instincts were directed elsewhere. 'Well, I must say, they look a rum lot, these refugees and dissidents, or whatever they are.' I said I thought the Muscovites probably said the same about Philby — not to mention Burgess and Maclean. 'Maybe,' he conceded. 'Maybe exile destroys people. That would be an interesting thing to discuss with him. Can an exile contribute to the literature of a country and a society he has abandoned for ever?' I obviously knew the scene, he went on. Did I think I could see that something sensible was arranged? There would be a small fee — research, he would call it. And I might even get a credit, which couldn't be bad could it? He laughed, said goodnight and skilfully pushed his way through to where Sue was talking to someone from the *Times Literary Supplement*, kissed her on the cheek and with a wave of the hand moved quickly through the door.

That was how I came to be in the BBC's Lime Grove studios with Boris Semyonov in tow. He did well, although in a truculent mood, which Colin dealt with cleverly, ducking the accusations about the decadence of Western intellectuals and leading Semyonov on to talk about his hopes and fears. His greatest fear, the writer said, was to look round and see his own steps in virgin snow: it made him feel like the last man left alive. His hope was to live and write in the greatest language on earth. It was Pushkin who said that only a great people could be worthy of such a great language. We would perhaps live to see his country and his people fulfill its historic and Christian mission in the world. The other interview was with a young ballerina who had just made a sensational début at Covent Garden; she had soft red hair and the pallor that often accompanies it. Afterwards we all met in the hospitality room with Colin, Sue and some of the crew. The drinks cupboard was open and there were the usual sandwiches to mop up some of the alcohol. Sue shortly made her apologies and left, not before reminding me that I was responsible for Semyonov. I said I didn't intend to play gooseberry and glanced over to where the poet was holding the dancer's hand and examining her legs. Sue shrugged. Shortly after she had left, Semyonov rose and announced that he and the young lady were 'going on — was that the right expression? — somewhere.' The dancer wrapped herself in a long knitted coat of many colours and allowed him to take her arm. As if on cue the members of the crew drank up and left. 'A marvellous show,' said Colin in valediction. 'Keep it up! See you next week! Thank you everybody!' He embraced the woman vision-mixer, who blushed. Then we were alone.

Colin leaned back in his chair and signalled to me to fill up the glasses. 'What will happen to the poor devil,' he wondered, 'when he loses touch with the great Russian language — and there's no doubt at all that it is a great language — none at all — when he gets tired of screwing young girls and needs more and more hooch to keep going? Do your people ever think of that?' I asked what on earth he meant by 'your

people'. 'I was only joking, dear boy, only joking,' he replied.
'But I must say I have always felt you should be in some sort
of cloak-and-dagger outfit.' 'Instead of which,' I said, 'here I
am, a citizen of Grub Street.' He found this amusing. 'Grub
Street — very good. I like that. Television is today's Grub
Street. Oliver Goldsmith would have been a TV natural — a
nature programme, don't you think? — didn't he write a
highly imaginative book about animals? — and chairman of
the Screenwriters Guild. Dr Johnson would have presided
over Mastermind. Can't you just see it? Sir, your ignorance
appals me. Or being interviewed by the *Radio Times*. Dr
Johnson, how do you see the role of questionmaster? A harmless drudge, sir, a harmless drudge. But you do quite well — I
mean enough to keep the wolf from the door. After all you
still edit some sort of review, don't you? But if you've any
programme ideas don't forget to let me know.' I nodded and
there was silence. 'Ever since I met him at that publisher's
party — by the way, isn't Sue's boss a creep? — I've been
absolutely fascinated by our friend, Semyonov. Why on earth
did he come to the West? I've been boning up on him naturally.
He wasn't doing badly — reading his poems to vast audiences
of young people. Getting published most of the time. I suppose
people like him take what they read in *Pravda* and *Izvestia* and
put it into reverse phase, so to speak. Positive for negative,
negative for positive. So they end up cheering any reactionary
government under the sun provided it makes sufficiently anti-
Soviet noises. I can understand it, of course — can't you? —
after all it's what we did ourselves in our salad days. At least I
did, I confess. In the thirties, I mean, when we thought that
because the capitalist press — which, God knows, was lying
through its teeth about many things — said the Moscow trials
were a farce, we thought they must be on the level, swallowed
the Moscow line and accepted all that nonsense about Trotskyite
wreckers. You remember? There was one high functionary
who was accused of putting glass in the butter! And the
purges, not to mention the suppression of the wretched kulaks.
I sometimes think,' he went on, for I made no comment, 'that

113

no generation was ever so duped, so conned as ours. Not only here. In Russia and Germany, too. Think of the poor buggers who went off to fight in the International Brigade or sweated their guts out selling the *Daily Worker* and collecting milk for Spanish children. Not that fighting Fascism was wrong — what was wrong were the lies pushed out to make us support a great and just cause. All the cover-ups about the GPU and how its executioners worked in Spain. The way that it became as good as a death sentence in Eastern Europe to have fought on the Republican side. And what about the young Germans? You had a year in Germany, didn't you? Have you ever wondered where your German fellow-students met their end? Stalingrad? Kursk? El Alamein? But of course one thing has to be said — no, two things. One is this. Whatever went wrong in Russia, whatever enormities Uncle Joe committed, the Russian people fought amazingly: if they hadn't, I don't suppose you and I would be here drinking the Beeb's whisky and remembering our youthful excesses.' 'And the other?' I asked curiously. 'The other? Ah yes. You can say what you like about Soviet Communism — you must remember that book by the Webbs: *Soviet Communism — A New Civilization.*' I said I did and reminded him that later editions had added a question mark after *Civilization*. Colin laughed. 'So they did. But anyway what I mean to say is that there was, to my mind, a fundamental difference between — what shall I call it? — the ethos underlying the system that Stalin distorted and the one Hitler invented. How to put it? Behind Soviet Communism there was at least a dream — Marx says somewhere that mankind has always had the dream of something — a utopia, if you like, the dream that people might some day escape from the inevitability of economic and other oppressions and enter — what did he call it? — the realm of freedom. Whereas what were the prospects with Hitler? Persecution, slave labour, racial extermination and perpetual warfare. I had a letter in my hands once — from Himmler — away back in the old days of the Army of the Rhine — which contemplated a frontier on the Urals across which the SS would carry on constant raids into Asia and so be blooded in perpetual warfare against racially inferior peoples. I don't know about you but I find this worse than anything Stalin dreamt up.' 'Including the Gulags?' I inquired. 'Damn it,' he exclaimed, 'you can't write off Socialism and its utopias like that or because of the iniquities committed in its name. You might as well write off Christianity because of the Inquisition and witch-burning. Racial persecution is part and parcel of Nazism, which is a creed it is impossible to distort. It is by its nature an iniquity.' We were both silent for a while. 'Were you ever a member of the Party?' he asked suddenly. I said No. 'I was for a while,' he continued, 'then I became disenchanted. It leaves a mark on you though. Having been a Party member.' He laughed and took some more whisky. 'Here I am talking as if you were my father confessor — or my shrink. I suppose it's because we know a good deal about each other. Come from the same neck of the woods, as they say. Did you ever think of going back to Scotland? I did. But I didn't think I could take it. Such a bloody anal society. Smug and self-satisfied. Here's tae us wha's like us. That sort of thing.' A security guard looked round the door, apologized and withdrew. Colin reflected for a while; I wondered how much further the whisky would loosen his tongue. 'But I could never bring myself to be a cold warrior, that's one thing. That's why I stopped doing things for the BBC's Overseas Services. You can — you still do bits and pieces for Bush House don't you?' 'Mostly cultural stuff,' I said almost defensively but he paid no attention, borne along by the liquor. 'Talking of cultural stuff, did you see that exhibition of dissident art from Eastern Europe at the ICA? Enough to make you weep. Phoney abstracts. Wretched sculpture. All that religiosity. With a touch of the Picassos to make it fashionable. Sometimes I can almost understand what Krushchev was on about when he denounced the stuff. Crap, dear boy, crap! But didn't the popular press love it! Because it fitted their Cold War mentality. Whereas when there is a decent exhibition of modern art they only cover it if there is something to guy. A thousand pounds for junk you could put

115

together in your own backyard! Waste of taxpayer's money. That sort of thing. I wanted to do a very critical bit about it but nobody was interested. Too negative, they said. Right, let's drink up or we shall be locked in for the night.' He insisted on driving me back to Hampstead although it was out of his way, his flat being in a splendid terrace overlooking Regent's Park. In the car I asked him whether he had ever thought of putting down on paper some of his thoughts of what it had been like to be a Communist in the thirties. Yes, indeed, he had. Frequently. Had made lots of notes but never seemed to get round to doing anything with them. I said I had always thought there was a book there somewhere and had done a certain amount of research — tape-recorded the odd interview with those who were prepared to speak about it. Didn't he feel he might have an interesting contribution to make? 'Perhaps, dear boy, perhaps,' was his answer. 'Why don't you give me a buzz one of these days and we can have a chat about it. Mind you — I'd have to be careful. I don't want Mr Gilchrist on my tail again.' It was, I knew, little more than a conventional gesture, a sign that he didn't want to be crudely rejecting; but it was something to work on. 'Right,' I said, 'I'll take you up on that.' 'Well,' he said with a laugh, as I directed him to draw up near my *dépendance*, 'this is a smart part of town for the residence of someone who labours in Grub Street.' And with a 'See you soon, dear boy, see you soon,' he drove off.

I leant forward and turned the sound down slightly as Colin appeared in shot, limping ever so slightly, from among huge, free-standing photographs of Old Russia — wooden churches, peasant women with head scarves — and began to talk about the tragedy of exile and the greatness of the Russian language as if he shared some sort of cultural home with the Slavs.

'I don't remember this stuff,' said Sue.

'I expect it's live,' I explained and turned up the volume. The programme was much as I remembered it in the studio. Semyonov's flaxen hair was unnaturally white under the lights;

116

his face had a strange beauty. A couple of clever edits had removed the one spot where his accent had been impossibly thick. Colin had a copy of *Flowers of Ice* in his hand. As he turned to camera to announce the celebrity he would interview next week I switched off. The image imploded to a dot of light and faded. Sue agreed that Colin had done the book proud — a copy well in shot — and went off into her little kitchen where she began to prepare what smelt like fish-fingers. I could hear Penelope, whose diet was more carefully arranged than Sue's own, slurping at her dish beside the sink. 'Did I tell you,' I asked disingenuously, 'that he has agreed to be interviewed?' There was a pause filled with the sizzle of frying fish. 'What on earth for? Not that book of yours? My God, did he really fall for it?' 'You know perfectly well I've done quite a bit of homework for it and I've got some leads. At any rate he said to ring — I think I'll give it a whirl.' Sue appeared with a tray. Fish fingers and some lettuce. 'I'll believe it when I see it,' she said. 'I can't think why you bother. What's so interesting about Colin Elphinstone anyway? If there really was anything on him it would have come out by now. Your friends in Curzon Street can't think he's very interesting. I mean, what do you think there is to dig up about him? Membership of the CP? He's no more devoted to red revolution than you or I. Or are you saying he's a sleeper planted in the media to destroy the moral fibre of that nation? Do you think he's done anything our masters don't know about?' 'Of course they know,' I replied. 'But they do nothing about it.' Sue pushed Penelope away from her tray with an impatient gesture and we ate in silencce. When we had finished she swept up the remains of the supper and from the kitchen almost shouted: 'I'm going to give you a word of warning. I'd watch out if I were you. This constant obsession. This fixation. You're jealous of him. Why? Because he was born with this silver spoon in his mouth — not a very big spoon — but a hell of a lot better than the electroplated one you got landed with. And that's simply too much for your lower middle class, small town, Presbyterian soul with its views about right and wrong. Your curious idea that there should be some sort of justice in this world which someone — Jehovah maybe? — should dole out. Fair shares for all and all that post-war crap. So you'll just have to come to terms with the facts of life, which are to do with stately homes and how beautiful they stand — '

'To prove the upper classes have still the upper hand.'

'Top marks. You're learning — even if Noel Coward is a tiny bit — shall I say frivolous? — coming from you. But forget that. What I'm warning you against is paranoia. It will eat you up, you know. And it will end badly. Once upon a time it would have worried me. Now I just find it boring. Now will you please go home — you never know there might be an invitation to drinkies — and let me get on with my work. I've got to read a typescript by some young man who made eyes at my boss at a dinner party.'

— Hello, Colin.

  — Who's this?

(The reply defensive)

  — John Melville.

  — John, dear boy, what have you been up to since our session at the studios?

  — Nothing much. Bits and pieces. The usual in fact.

(The pause expectant)

  — I'm ringing about the book I mentioned in the car that night.

  — Remind me, dear boy. I've a rather vague —

  — A book about politics in the armed forces. And what made people join the Communist Party in the thirties.

(The silence unresponsive)

  — As I said I've talked to some people but I have a hunch you might —

  — Dear boy, I'm sure I've got much —

  — It wouldn't take long. Say a couple of hours on tape.

  — I've rather a lot —

  — I just thought that with your knowledge of the scene —

(The fly of flattery drawn over the fish)

— I'm just off on a recce. I've got this big series coming up in the autumn so I'm a bit pushed just at the moment. So why don't I get in touch when I get back. I expect it will keep.

(The bait refused. The cold shoulder. The frozen mitt.)

— Okay then. We'll be in touch. You haven't got a date in mind?

— Afraid not — you know what it's like. But keep in touch, dear boy, keep in touch. By the way, where did you get my number? It's supposed to be ex-directory.

— From Sue Godwin actually.

(Astonished silence)

— She didn't think you'd mind. Between old friends, so to speak.

— Of course not. Ciao.

Actually Sue had been furious for I had got it by rummaging in her handbag and extracting her address-book, that essential weapon in her fight for existence. She caught me red-handed, called me a shit and wanted to know what I was going to do with it. 'You know what I'm going to do with it. I'm going to ring him at home one of these days so that that bloody secretary of his can't stymie me. He'll talk. He's vain enough.'

'That's for sure — but I doubt if he'll talk,' she countered. 'I think it's a waste of time.'

I first heard about the tunnel from Gilchrist. It was, I imagined, some sort of quid pro quo for the hint I had given about the Schneider affair. He had been missing from Grace's for some days — 'fishing', said Malcolm, which meant, for his money, visiting his old folk who had retired to Aviemore where they cannily supplemented their pensions with the income from bed and breakfast. When Gilchrist reappeared, however, it was not with his usual stories of salmon that got away with flies, cast and all, or slipped from the gaff just when he was

119

about to land his catch in the net. For once he was uncom-
municative and would go no further than say that he had been
abroad on an assignment. Towards the end of the afternoon,
however, as the drink began to loosen his tongue, he suddenly
became confidential. 'Jock,' he said, with his face so close to
mine that I could see each enlarged pore on his nose, 'Jock,
you're a tight, secure, buttoned-up sort of bloke. If I tell you
something will you promise you'll not go off and sell it down
the Street?' I must have looked annoyed for he hastened to
pacify me. 'Jesting, my friend, merely jesting. What's yours?
A drap o' the auld Kirk? Right.' He waited until Malcolm had
served us and moved away before he spoke. 'You know
Berlin don't you?' I said I hadn't been there for a while. 'You
should go, laddie, you should go. It's a hell of a place. For a'
kinds o' things. From spies to blue movies. With your connections you would have a hell of a time, What's that? You've
nae connections? We understand each other. Mum's the word.
Now listen to this.' He gave a quick glance to where Grace
and Malcolm were debating how to place their money on the
4.30 at Doncaster. 'There's a plan afoot — in fact it's begun —
to dig a tunnel under the Wall. Jesus man, what a story. A
trap-door to freedom. I tell you there's been nothing like it
since the big breakouts from German POW camps during
war.' 'The Wooden Horse, Mark II,' I suggested. 'Aye, the
Wooden Horse. Colditz. That sort of thing. I had it from an
American TV cameraman. One of the kind that has more than
one job — wink wink nudge nudge. Anyway he's promised
me an exclusive for Britain. With stills of the first people
coming through. The first breath of freedom — what a head-
line! It'll cost a bawbee or two, of course, but I think yours
truly can probably get the editor to cough up. It'll take a wee
while naturally. The East German pollis have listening equipment. So canny's the word. Look — it's like this.' He produced
an envelope and proceeded to show how the tunnel started
from a basement in the East, ran out under no-man's-land and
would eventually connect with a tunnel from the West complete with phones, lighting and all that. They were going to

120

tip him the wink when the tunnel was almost complete and he would fly in for the great moment. 'But for Jesus' sake keep it under your hat. I'm only telling you because you're as tight as a wee virgin. Not that there's many of them about these days. Incidentally I saw our mutual friend, Elphinstone, in Berlin with a film-crew. He had the nerve to come up to me in a bar and ask if I'd invented any good stories lately. I said I'd get him yet. He laughed and said he looked forward to reading the piece. Said he always read me. I was almost as exciting as James Bond only not quite so well written. The saucy bastard. If you get any more on him, will you slip a word into my ear. By the way it seems he's gone freelance. I should think that's a load off the Beeb's mind. Said he was making a film about lost paintings — the ones Hitler destroyed. Degenerate, they were called apparently. For what it's worth — and of course I'm only a laddie from up a tenement close that never went to college but I've seen some of the stuff — I think Hitler was maybe right for once.' We pledged secrecy in some straight malts and he left to put the screws on the old man at the papers.

It was Sue who persuaded me to go that autumn to the International Writers' Congress in Yugoslavia. I objected that I wasn't really a writer. She replied that a lot of other people there wouldn't be writers either so I wouldn't be odd man out. After all I was a regular broadcaster and journalist and what about that book I was supposed to be working on — radical politics in the armed forces in World War II — wasn't that it? I didn't respond to that thrust so she went on across my silence to say her boss was too mean to send her and — given his antecedents as an ex-Monarchist Yugoslav exile not too keen on going anyway — but she was sure I'd find funds for the trip somehow and I could let her know what went on. In return she'd see if there was anyone — Radio Three perhaps — who might take a piece on the Congress.

Landing at Belgrade on a hot autumn evening I found the city lying under a layer of smog that rested in the streets just at

121

head height. The acrid fumes stung the eyes and settled in hair and clothes. At dinner in my hotel they drifted in through the top of the high windows like a mist. It came, someone said knowledgeably, from burning low-grade Rumanian oil. The service was slow and the food uninspired but in the bar afterwards the slivovitz was oily, fragrant and potent. A few local girls waited to be picked up at the bar or at the tables. No doubt payment would be expected in hard currency. At my side an American in a smart light-weight suit eyed them with interest. Turning to me he enquired whether I was by any chance going to this writers' congress. He professed himself delighted to learn that I was. In his strong New York accent he explained that he had never before been behind the Iron Curtain. So far he had not been impressed. The smog was worse than L.A. The food was revolting. And look at the way the hookers were dressed. Still it was reassuring that the oldest profession flourished even here. He had heard there were even strip-clubs. Strippers behind the Iron Curtain, wasn't that something? Did I feel like going to see what we could find? I excused myself: I had been up very early and we had another early start next morning and a long coach trip to our destination in the mountains. Belatedly he introduced himself. Henry Greenspan, editor of *Rubric*. I might have heard of it. Did I know *Encounter* in the UK? Well, he reckoned *Rubric* was better — with more of an edge to it — and especially well-informed on Eastern Europe and Arab-Israeli relations. What had my name been again? Was I a writer or just an observer? A bit of both, I said, but I was I supposed really a political journalist and broadcaster. He flatteringly claimed to know of the *Review*, by reputation at least. People he knew who contributed to *Rubric* and whose judgement he trusted had told him it was a very sound publication, highly informed but just — if I'd forgive his frankness — just a tiny bit dull. In general, he went on, he found that in Europe people were rather soft — too inclined to pull their punches — to think that the bureaucrats who ran people's lives in the East were reasonable human beings like themselves. He was persuaded that they were not.

122

He paused and watched curiously as one of the girls concluded a deal with a German businessman. What, he wondered, was the price of a piece of ass behind the Iron Curtain? That would make a nice odd-ball piece for the scrapbook column of *Rubric*, didn't I think? He'd see I got a copy — maybe I'd find it useful enough to take out a subscription. I had another slivovitz while he said goodnight and went off on some voyage of discovery in the sultry, fume-laden dark.

We sat together in the coach next day as we drove through the mountains of Hercegovina. Greenspan marvelled at everything: at the women in the fields in their baggy, flowered trousers, at the mosque in Sarajevo, at the great synagogue opposite across the river, at the men sitting Middle Eastern fashion in little bars by the roadside. It was as if he had expected to confront a landscape out of a science-fiction movie, inhabited by some race of sub-human helots. I made a remark about the deceptive ordinariness of oppressed societies. He asked if he might use that in the piece he was going to do about the Congress; to which I assented since it wasn't original in the first place. As the bus climbed up through the high gorges, hesitating on the bends, skirting the verge so that one had the impression of hanging over the void, I remembered that Colin had been dropped somewhere hereabouts in 1943. The forests, the cliffs and the high bare grasslands showed no trace of the fighting. Once or twice the name of a village stirred some memory from accounts of the grinding battle as Tito's rearguards strove to hold the river-line — perhaps the very river I could see far below if I peered from the window — and allow the main body to cross and reform in the fastnesses of Montenegro. In spite of his initial fears over the competence of the driver, the efficacy of the brakes and the condition of the road, Greenspan had fallen asleep, perhaps exhausted by his nocturnal wanderings. He woke only when the coach drove up in front of our hotel, a rambling, old-fashioned building that clearly dated back to the Austro-Hungarian Empire, when the summer visitors from Vienna and Trieste had used to come to take the waters and stroll in parasoled couples by the

123

lake. The mountains rose sharply beyond the water. The islands were dark with pines. There was a tang of pine-needles in the air.

The party debussed in a slightly confused way and picked over the luggage which the porters, in their traditional green aprons and shirt-sleeves, deposited in the foyer. Slowly we found our pieces. There was immediately a queue at the reception desk. What if they asked for his passport? Greenspan inquired. He had no intention of letting them have it. It was well known they would simply take it away and copy it. For obvious reasons. But the receptionist merely looked at it, checked the name from a list, and returned it with a smile. 'Mr Greenspan,' the accent was unmistakably American, 'Room 202. Welcome to Zelena Gora. I hope you enjoy your vacation, sir.' When I came down from my room the line at the desk had almost entirely thinned out. There was still some luggage lying in the middle of the foyer with, next to it, a new accretion — a heap of film equipment. A couple of English technicians stood guard over it and — experts on hotels over most of the world — wondered if the present dump would be up to their standards. I asked if they were BBC or ITV. Neither, they explained, they were a freelance crew working for an independent producer. A chap called Elphinstone. They were going to cover some sort of writers' conference. I said I knew Elphinstone a little. They thought he'd be back soon, he'd just gone to sort out a little problem with the manager. They had actually expected himself — the cameraman — and his assistant to share a room and there was no way they were going to do that. It was separate rooms or they packed up and forget about the conference. They reckoned it would be all right though, Elphinstone seemed to speak the lingo and had some sort of pull with these people. But filming behind the Iron Curtain — forgive his French — was a pain in the arse. No night life. Bad food. You could keep socialism as far as he was concerned.

Colin, when he appeared, was too occupied with soothing the camera crew to notice me where I stood near the huge,

124

leisurely, creaking brass-gated lift. It was only when he had completed negotiations at the desk that he looked up and saw me. As usual he greeted me with what seemed real pleasure; there was nothing to suggest that he remembered the slight coldness of our last telephone conversation some months back. 'Well, this is a turn up for the book — meeting you in Zelena Gora. I'm covering the Congress. It should be interesting, don't you think? Writers and journalists from east and west. I want to do some interviews. There'll be readings and what our French friends call cultural manifestations. But the really interesting thing will be to talk to people here in Yugoslavia, which is a sort of Tom Tiddler's ground, don't you think? I have a hunch tongues might be a little less guarded than they would be, in, say, Prague or Budapest or Warsaw. I'd like to get the flavour of it all. With this to provide the pictorial values, as they say.' He pointed out to where the mountains were beginning to throw a shadow on the lake and turn the water black. 'And the hotel, of course. Isn't it terribly Franz Josef? I shouldn't be surprised to hear that it's haunted by the Archduke who got himself shot in Sarajevo. He used to come up here to slaughter wild animals.' We made a date to meet for dinner. In my bedroom there was a pile of literature: details of seminars, of recitals, of folk-dancing displays, official receptions. Lists of delegates and observers. Under the German Democratic Republic I was interested to see the name of Hermann Schneider and wondered if it was the Hermann Schneider I knew. There was also apparently an international chess championship which delegates were welcome to attend. And indeed, going down for a belated drink at the bar, I saw two players, watched by a small group of professionals and what looked like their trainers — or minders — fighting out a game of high-speed chess with a rattle of pieces that reminded me of the noise of the backgammon boards in the Arab cafés of Cairo. I found Greenspan at a table on a terrace at the back of the lounge. He waved to me to join him. 'They are Russians,' he said, 'you can tell by their jackets. There's something about them that says they're not part of Western culture. Talking of

125

which,' he went on with an irony that was only half-mocking, 'did you know there was a casino here — with striptease. A casino — no doubt a relic of imperial decadence — *and* strippers. Maybe the system is beginning to crack.'

It was inevitable that he should join Colin and me for dinner and equally inevitable, I suppose, that they should tangle with one another. Colin was patient when Greenspan, learning that he was a documentary film-maker working in television — something he never watched himself because he thought the term idiot's lantern very apt — said that in his view documentary film-makers were usually radicals of one sort or another, from liberal to socialist. He wasn't at all sure they should have what sometimes looked like the free run of a mass medium, where one had absolutely no idea who the audience were or how capable its members were of construing accurately what appeared on the screen. He didn't have much time for Marshall McLuhan, who was a confused Catholic populist — sloppy in argument and inaccurate in his references — but certainly the idea of the electronic village was a striking and frightening one. He interrupted his statement, which he delivered with extraordinary fluency, to inquire whether there was some more interesting fruit than apples and grapes. Colin said something to the waiter, who gave a slight bow and returned with a bowl of figs, which Greenspan began to peel warily, wondering whether they had heard about washing fruit in Jugoslavia. 'How come you speak Serbo-Croat? I assume that's what it was,' he remarked as if he had only now understood how Colin had intervened. I explained that during the war Colin had very likely been in those mountains across the lake, which were now greying as the sun sank behind them. 'This was the headquarters of a German mountain division, this hotel,' said Colin. 'We were up there.' He pointed to where above the dark masses of the pines steep grassy slopes ran up to the precipitous ramparts of a distant plateau. 'Zelena Gora,' he explained, 'the green hill. You could look down through field-glasses and see the despatch-riders and staff-cars come and go. If you have time — and inclination — I suggest

126

you drive to the head of the lake. There's a monument there — actually it's the bare foundations of village houses. The Germans and their allies, the Chetniks — the right-wing Yugoslav collaborators — destroyed the village and killed the entire population, men, women and children, on the grounds that they supported the partisans.' I remembered another conversation with an American officer in Berlin twenty years before, and to avoid a repetition of that evening said I'd heard he had been in Berlin recently; which was a tactical error for Greenspan at once wanted to know what Berlin was like. He was going there after the Congress, via Vienna because he was leery of unnecessary travel behind the Curtain. He thought of it as an essential bastion of the West, which must at all costs be maintained, and no doubt a very exciting place to see. Colin agreed. It was very interesting. The Kurfuerstendamm was, he supposed, a showpiece for the West and for a society that had elevated the consumption of often unnecessary goods to a sacred doctrine. Did he think then, asked Greenspan truculently, that what was by all accounts the grey uniformity of the other side of the wall was preferable? 'Well,' said Colin, surprisingly coolly, 'it may not be everybody's cup of tea — as we British say — neither East Berlin nor the German Democratic Republic, but may I remind you that there is every sign that the standard of living of the population is rising, that there is a policy of good cheap housing and transport, and that of all the examples of existing socialism, the GDR is the only one that did not have bloody purges — even in Stalin's day. All that seems to speak for it. To a certain extent at least.' Greenspan objected that there had been the June rising of 1954, by the workers, who didn't seem to be impressed by the regime. 'Even that,' Colin replied, 'didn't have the sort of bloody aftermath that followed the Hungarian uprising.' That apart, he thought that but for an immense subsidy from Bonn — and elsewhere — West Berlin would simply wither and die. Greenspan wanted to know if this meant that Colin was prepared to hand the West Berliners over to the East, lock, stock and barrel, although there was plenty of evidence that brave men and women were

127

prepared to die on the Wall trying to escape to a society where there was at least something to consume. 'Let me tell you something,' said Colin. 'Some of the escapees are no doubt genuine. Some of them just don't like the work ethic of the GDR. Some of them want a bit of adventure and are manipulated by people with money — hard currency. Others are agents and the tools of agents.' 'The CIA again?' asked Greenspan ironically. 'Maybe — it wouldn't surprise me — would it you?' Colin continued. 'But actually I am thinking of an American television network. You know the television world is really very small, full of gossip but often highly informed. The word is among the television people in West Berlin that there is a ploy on foot to tunnel under the Berlin Wall and — wait for it — have live pictures of the escapees as they come up into the Western way of life. The great break for freedom will find its place alongside some soap opera or whatever is prime time viewing on the channel. I'll wager that high-powered executives on the rival channel are even now agonizing over the great decision whether it is worth putting their money into a second tunnel in the name of competition, the free market and democracy. I don't know about you but it makes me sick. And now if you'll excuse I think I'll turn in. I have an early call tomorrow.' Greenspan watched him go in silence then turned to remark: 'If this had been a poker game he'd have been pretty unpopular, walking out on me like that. What is this friend of yours anyway? One of those upper-class British Commies we keep hearing about or what?' I found myself arguing perversely that in terms of the British class system Colin wasn't actually upper class but Greenspan wasn't interested. 'I think I'll take in the casino,' he said. 'You coming along?'

The casino was like the set for a German feature film of the twenties, with a doorkeeper swathed in gold braid, girls in fish-net stockings in the cloakroom and, over the gaming tables, a cloud of tobacco smoke as thick and pungent as Belgrade's petrol fumes. We watched the roulette for a few minutes. Greenspan wanted to know if I didn't feel like putting some money on one of the colours but I said it went against my Presbyterian grain and that, in any case, I only had to lay money on a horse in the Grand National for it to fall at the first fence. Greenspan laughed for the first time since we met and said I should have known his old man in the Bronx who pawned a menorah once — did I know what a menorah was? — and lost the money on some bob-tailed nag in the Kentucky Derby. 'That leaves sex,' he went on and led the way through the gaming-room to where a dejected-looking band in plum-coloured uniforms with silver facings waited for the audience to take its place on spidery gilt chairs round a small square dance-floor, while the waiters scurried about with drinks. With surprising agility Greenspan snapped up a couple of places by the very edge of the floor, under the nose of a French delegate with a pile of white candy-floss hair above an aquiline nose and a companion who wore over her arm an equally white and highly shampooed dog. They moved disdainfully to the other side of the room. Greenspan beckoned a waiter and ordered a couple of Scotches, which cost an inordinate number of dinars, but then, he commented philosophically, one had to expect to be fleeced in a clip-joint either side of the Curtain. They had scarcely arrived when there was a roll of drums from the orchestra, the curtains at the back of the dance-floor opened and a woman emerged, not tall but opulent, with dyed black hair and the kind of white skin I associated with Victorian paintings of slave-girls. She wore a green silk coat which with calculated negligence she allowed to open to show beneath it a green brassière, green stockings secured with red garters and rather old-fashioned French knickers. The green light, reflected on her skin, gave it a curiously gangrenous tinge. In her naval was a large red paste gem. When the drum-roll died away there was a scatter of applause, which she acknowledged with a slight bow before the band struck up *The Blue Danube* and the performance began. She was soon well into the banal routine, tearing at her long green gloves with her teeth in simulated passion, ogling Greenspan, whom she mutely invited to tug at the cord that secured her

129

cloak, and then dancing away from him with a motion of her buttocks and belly which was, he whispered, her best feature. It reminded me of the dancing-girls of Cairo. Indeed so strong was the resemblance that I half expected to hear her break into a song with a long melisma, like the ones that used to set the smart Egyptian army officers laughing but left the occupation troops impatient and unamused, half-suspecting they were the butts of the laughter. The Turks, I reminded Greenspan, had been in these parts for a very long time; but he seemed not to hear me, being caught up in the ritual as she unhooked her brassière and, with feigned coyness, released her breasts. His face had that curiously withdrawn look I had seen so often before on the faces of the exiles and defectors whom, at Sue's request, I introduced to Soho and their new freedoms. The band struck up a tune that also went back to my Cairo days, *Deep is the Night* — cannibalized Chopin, Yvette had called it — dug up from some improbable repertoire. To its slow rhythm she undulated about the dance-floor making coy gestures towards the waistband of her knickers. The music stopped. She stepped out of them with extraordinary agility and for a second stood there in a spangled cache-sex with the paste gem glowing in her navel. The lights cut out. There was some applause at which she emerged from the curtains once more in her cloak and acknowledged it haughtily. Greenspan was saying something about having seen better in Bourbon Street, New Orleans, when, over the heads of the audience, I caught sight of Schneider. He was standing by the entrance, looking disdainfully — as it seemed to me — at the whole scene. He turned away. I excused myself and made towards him. He had gone towards the gaming room. I followed, lost him, mistook an opening and found myself suddenly in a kitchen where a couple of chefs looked up with surprise from their saucepans. I turned back and reached the cloakroom. But he was not there. Outside in the long drive to the casino I was just in time to see the tail lights of a large official car wink as it turned a corner and was hidden by some trees.

Over the next few days I saw Colin only rarely. Usually he greeted me from a distance as, followed by his PA — his latest 'Sue' — who read his mind, transmitted his instructions, attended to his needs — did she, I wondered, also sleep with him? — and by a retinue of technicians, he moved through the plenary session and the succeeding seminars, shooting close-ups of distinguished delegates, climbing on to the platform for shots of the audience and shepherding an élite to be inter-viewed in a side room which — no doubt using that pull he had with the authorities — he had commandeered as his base: all this with his lordly way that brooked no refusal. I was irresistibly reminded of the assurance with which long ago he had marshalled the speakers at those Edinburgh meetings of the Left Book Club, the British Youth Peace Assembly or the Friends of the Soviet Union. Since the dinner with Greenspan we had not exchanged more than a few words on odd occasions, one of them at a buffet lunch where he darted off in mid-sentence, abandoning a half-eaten sandwich, to capture the French delegate whom he charmed away from his companion and her dog and led off to face the camera. But his moments of greatest activity followed the arrival of an American author, whose wife's body was the erotic focus of almost the entire world and whose absences was like an indefinable presence — as if he still had about him the warmth and perfume of her skin. He was a great prize and to his capture Colin devoted his total energies. His aim he achieved only after overcoming a certain resistance, inspired — so Colin indicated during a brief interval in the chase — by none other than Greenspan; but in the end persistence and the dropping of a couple of names from the New York art world ended the chase. It followed that I never succeeded in putting to him the question that recurred obsessively in my thoughts: How many other people had he told of the tunnel? Who else knew? Did he make a habit of blurting the information out to strangers like Greenspan or in the course of after-dinner conversations with friends and acquaintances? (What category, I wondered, did I fall into?) It was true that in a sense both Greenspan and I were safe

131

repositories of such secrets: Greenspan because of his ideological commitment and myself because he knew I had had long training in the handling of even more secret and dangerous information. But if he knew, how many others did in the bars and hotel bedrooms of Berlin where the media men sat and drank, loaded their film-cameras, played back their tapes or typed their stories, and how secure were they? Perhaps they too, because of a certain professional discretion, were safe recipients, like Gilchrist, jealously guarding nuggets of information which in due course they would use to get a beat on their rivals and so win an approving phone call from their news editors. Meantime deep under no-man's-land the tunnellers scraped at the stubborn strata of rubble, earth and mud, hauled up the spoil and somehow disposed of it in secret. Two, three, — maybe four men or women with motives which — here I had to agree with Colin — might be mixed, impure, even suspect, who stopped their work and lay scarcely breathing when they fancied they heard a noise overhead and cursed under their breath if their implements rang on a stone. Gilchrist — with that unerring nose for cliché, which was the reason for his professional success — had drawn the parallel with the Oflag escapes of World War II; but here the penalties for being caught were not just a spell in the cooler and there would be no benign, stiff-lipped Senior British Officer to welcome them at the end of their time inside. At the other end of the tunnel the camera crews waited in relays, grumbling a little no doubt at the boredom which they fought by reading comics, playing poker and totting up their overtime. Up above, the man or woman — for there was not likely to be more than one — who was the liaison between the two ends of the tunnel came and went by S-Bahn or simply walked through at Checkpoint Charlie. Someone so motivated or so calculating that he or she was prepared to risk the suspicious notice of the state security police and rendezvous — where? — in a safe flat or in a bar or café with the director who was no innocent at the game, having — as Gilchrist put it — more than one job, who had a budget and knew precisely, when it came to haggling, just how much that person's services were worth.

Greenspan, too, was elusive. One morning, sitting in on a session on *Structures and Poetics*, I found him in full flow, delivering an attack on what he called 'the formalistic fallacy' which he defined as a lack of concern for the content of literary works. There were, to judge from some of the contributions he had heard in the course of the present seminar, persons whom one might have expected — particularly at a congress taking place where it did on the ideological frontiers of Europe — to acknowledge the presence of a cultural world beyond the literary work and a cultural system beyond the literary one. He did not quarrel — he went on with his extraordinary fluency and his ability, speaking impromptu, to formulate his thoughts with precision and eloquence — he did not quarrel with the view that the purely formal description of literary works and literary systems was an important activity. The fallacy, he insisted, lay in the refusal to acknowledge that these were not the only aspect that required our attention, or in the equally wrongheaded insistence that these aspects function in an entirely closed system without influence from the world beyond literature. If the students of structures — which some speakers proposed as closed non-referential systems — insisted in being cut off in a formal prison he doubted that they would have much to say to writers who were aware of that Iron Curtain, which delegates were so anxious should not be mentioned in their discussions or allowed to cast a shadow on their debates and junketings. Structuralism, if it was to be worthy of respect, must seek to explore the relationship between the system or systems of literature and the culture of which it is inevitably a part. When he sat down there was a stir in the assembly room. An East German delegate rose to denounce what he described as the American delegate's typical cold warrior's speech and his attempt, from which he was sure the others present would wish to disassociate themselves, to introduce a discordant note into a congress dedicated to the concept of friendship and peace — in the arts and literature as well as in other spheres. As he rose to his feet he uncovered to

133

my line of vision the unmistakable profile and white hair of Schneider, who when he sat down bent over and with a smile said something into his ear. The French delegate, for his part, made a slight but unequivocal inclination of the head — nod would have been altogether too coarse a term to describe it — towards Greenspan, who acknowledged the gesture of solidarity with a tiny motion of the hand, like a bidder at a high-class auction. From that day on when Greenspan was not paying homage among the courtiers who surrounded the famous American writer, they tended to sit together and eat together while Greenspan held forth in loud, accurate but strongly American French.

Schneider was billed to give a reading of his poems to which I duly went. He failed to turn up, his place being taken by a young man who read some blandly optimistic verses in which a vaguely pantheistic celebration of nature was accompanied by unexceptionable social statements about peace and love. From time to time boredom drove me from sessions where the very language — or the discourse, as I had learned to call it — was unfamiliar and densely obscure, to seek a diversion at the international chess tournament. Here the contestants confronted each other on a raised dais with, above it, an electronic chess board on which the moves were registered. I had not imagined that chess could involve such tension or such a display of physical energy as that which caused one of the champions to pace the platform between moves, going to and fro, oblivious of the audience, with quick sidelong glances at the board as he passed and in his movements the concentrated tension of a caged animal. The audience was scattered through the hall; its members came and went on tip-toe like churchgoers entering or leaving during the service; when they had chosen their places they concentrated on their little pocket chessboards with all the intensity of devout believers with their prayer-books. Occasionally at some especially daring or skilful move there came a slight sussuration of approval or surprise. At the front of the hall I recognized the trainers and minders whom I had seen that first evening watching the players rattle their pieces in the hotel lounge. It was no surprise one afternoon to see Schneider standing at the side of the dais, in close and prolonged conversation with one of the trainers, whom, I felt sure, my Hungarian acquaintance from Sue's publishing parties would have firmly identified as a member of the KGB. Their conversation over, Schneider sat for a few minutes to watch the game. As he left the hall he walked down the gangway between the chairs, passing within a couple of feet of me; he gave me a glance devoid of recognition and passed on. I did not see him again until the last night of the congress, marked by a reception in a villa by the lake to which, it seemed, the President himself came from time to time in imperial style to shoot chamois on Zelena Gora. In the pre-revolutionary splendour of the reception rooms the orchestra, tucked away in an alcove by the dance floor lined with potted palms, played a potpouri of vaguely folk melodies that gave way to a Strauss waltz for which delegates, soberly dressed but unmistakably of the present, with the air of men who had decided to humour their great, powerful if absent host, chose their partners from among the women delegates, the congress secretaries and translators, the congress wives, companions, mistresses or girlfriends, and took the floor. The French delegate's companion, tall, slim and slightly scraggy but undeniably chic, swept past in the arms of a huge Slav with a bush of greying hair in which some wound had traced a white furrow. I struggled through to the buffet where the delegates were jostling as if the deliberations of the last session, presided over by a hero of the partisan struggle in a dark suit and grey tie, with its fudged resolutions, its interminable speeches of thanks, its exhortations to international co-operation and friendship had sharpened their appetites enormously. Colin's crew was there too; having filmed the prettier delegates and the girls in national costume who served at the long tables, they themselves now pushed into the press, where the wine and slivovitz bore witness to generosity commensurate with the splendour of the setting. They were flying out next day and on to an assignment in

Thailand — not with Colin who was going back to London — relieved to see the last of Yugoslavia. I left them to forage and went in search of him. We were within a few feet of each other and he had acknowledged my approach over the heads of those around him, when with a roar the big Slav who, having abandoned his partner at the end of the waltz, burst through, seized Colin in his arms and lifted him off the floor in a long embrace. The bystanders fell back and watched with a mixture of curiosity, surprise and amusement, as he cleared a path to the liquor and the two men proceeded to drink a deep fraternal toast. I turned away, for clearly there was no possibility of intruding on the laughter, the exclamations in Serbo-Croat, the toasts and the embraces that united them. From the tall windows in one of the smaller drawing-rooms I looked out on to the lake and watched the fish nose to the surface and dimple the water. Occasionally one would leap almost clear and splash back, leaving concentric rings that silvered in the moonlight. I was overcome by a sensation of melancholy, which the slivovitz accentuated, of complete loneliness, a feeling that I had no reason to be there, no aim, no goal, no profession except that of scavenging crumbs of gossip and rumour, of scrabbling in Grub Street. I had none of Colin's romantic notions, no passionate commitment to equal Greenspan's, none of the drive and courage of the tunnellers up there in Berlin — only a deep scepticism about human motives and a pervading distrust of enthusiasm. Returning every so often to the bar to replenish my glass, I wandered through the less frequented rooms, exchanged a greeting with Greenspan who sat with the French couple, talking loudly, a little flushed with wine. Through an open French window I stepped out into the gardens that ran down to the lake. There was a terrace with a balustrade of rustic wood from which one could look clear up the lake over its islands to where Colin's Green Hill rose abruptly from the water. I paused on the flight of wooden steps and wondered how I would have borne myself had I been there among the hardships and cruelties of the partisan war. As I moved lower, I was aware of two men standing leaning on the railing, talking quietly together. Even

136

in the dark Schneider's white hair was unmistakable; the other was Colin. At the sound of my footsteps they looked round and stopped talking. I walked on. 'John, this is Hermann Paul Schneider, the East German poet. Why do I say that — damn it — the German poet. You may remember you met years ago in Hamburg.' Schneider gave a curt nod. 'We were just remarking how beautiful it was — the lake, Zelena Gora — and hoping it might never again be touched by war.' I made some sort of non-commital response and we chatted a little about the congress. Schneider was mostly mute. Then we walked awkwardly back into the villa where Colin explained that he had accepted a lift from Schneider but no doubt we would see each other on the plane next day. Schneider made no attempt to extend the offer of a lift to me but took his leave with his characteristic slight inclination of the head and body. From a window I watched them climb into the official car which went slowly up the drive with a creak of tyres on the gravel. There was still some slivovitz left at the bar. I drank until the lights began to go down and the last guests drifted towards the doors. Walking back along the lakeside I felt the breeze cool on my face but it did little to clear my mind in which the question persisted: What had been the true subject of their conversation and how had it continued in the official car?

Characteristically, Colin was travelling first as opposed to my tourist class. But halfway to Vienna he came back down the plane and sat beside me for a few minutes. He was in a communicative mood. The Slav who had embraced him was Ivo Rankovich, one of the giants — literally and metaphorically — of the partisan war. He still had a German bullet in his head. He had been rearguard commander in the break out of encirclement. If Colin — and Tom Pressman — got out alive it was thanks to Ivo. He seemed to be finding it difficult to fit in to the new order. He and Tito didn't see eye to eye on internal — not foreign policy — and Ivo was being marginalized. It was really rather sad. Colin looked out for a few seconds at the rolling floor of cloud. Then he laughed. 'Old Greenspan didn't like me much, did he? But what a monster. I don't think there's tuppence difference between him and some of his counterparts on the other side. A pity — he's not stupid. Very bright, in fact. Tell me, how can anyone so bright be so reactionary in his politics?' 'What's wrong with Schneider?' I asked abruptedly. What did I mean by 'wrong'? I said I found him bloody rude. Colin agreed — he could be abrupt — he had a bit of a chip, but there were long and complicated reasons. But he was okay once you got to know him. I let that pass, resolving instead to profit from the curious intimacy of conversation at twenty thousand feet. Did he remember that I wanted to tape him? Okay — he hadn't been able to for one reason or another — but couldn't we set something up again? Next week say. He thought for a moment then said right. Wednesday next. His place. 49 Regent's Terrace. Top floor. Five thirty. The stewardess's voice announced that we would shortly be landing at Vienna, ordered passengers back to their seats and went into the litany of orders preceding landing. 'Until the aircraft has come to a complete standstill and the engines have been switched off. Amen.' parroted Colin. Still he thought he had better comply — he had often wondered what would happen if one just ignored these phoney voices with their simulated caring, their totally bogus thanks for flying with them.

'I bet he finds some pressing reason to cancel,' was Sue's comment as we opened the duty-free booze together. 'I don't trust Master Colin further than I can throw him. You'll see.'

'I think maybe you're wrong. At all events I've been boning up on him.'

'I thought you knew it all already.'

'Most of it — but you never know.'

Elphinstone Colin b. 1917 s of James Elphinstone DSO MC

138

WS MP (deceased) and Mary Erskine (deceased).
Educated Fettes College, Magdalen College, Oxon, Edinburgh
University. The Courtauld Institute.
War Service: commissioned 1 Glasgow Highlanders; Long
Range Desert Group; British Military Mission to Yugoslavia;
GHQ Mediterranean Land Forces (GSO2); HQ 21 Army
group (GSO1); HQ British Army of the Rhine. MC DSO
1950-54 Lecturer in History of Art, Royal College of Art.
1954-60 Talks Department, BBC Television. Since 1960
freelance writer and film-maker.
Publications: *The Bare Mountain* (an account of partisan war
in Yugoslavia);
Robert Adam's Adriatic Journey (a study of the origins of
neoclassicism);
The Glass Eye (on the aesthetics of film and television).
Club: The Garrick. Hobbies: Travel. Watching old films.
m. Diana Pomfret Carter 1941. Marriage dissolved 1950.

Note omission: Should read: m. 1 Agnes Moir 1 son. Marriage
dissolved 1940, m. 2 Diana etc.

As he led the way from the door of the Regent's Terrace flat,
I noticed that his limp was quite marked. Perhaps he was
tired; perhaps at home his defences were allowed to slip.
While he got the drinks I looked round at the tall, classical
room with its egg-and-dart frieze and wondered when it
would be featured in one of the Sunday colour supplements
as an example of gracious living. Did he share it with anyone?
I wondered. There were no obvious signs and Sue thought
probably not. If he had women visitors she would bet it was
for a night, for a weekend, but not much longer. Why? Because
he felt safer that way. On the road round the park beneath the
windows, the lights of the homing cars made a red chaplet. I
thought I could hear the noise of animals somewhere in the
dusk. He must have heard it, too, for he made a remark about
how they could keep one awake at night — especially the
wolves. He poured a large whisky and we sat and drank and
chatted.

'Certainly I remember the match. You beat me four and one and then apologized most touchingly. Said something about practically living on the links. It must have been the hols before I went up to Oxford. Where did you go?'

'Edinburgh.'

'Of course! Rectorial elections and filming in the Old Quad! I had expected Edinburgh to be very staid and god-fearing. Instead it was quite bohemian and rather fun. God, doesn't it feel a long time ago. Like another world. All these naïve hopes. And you read? Don't tell me — German! I'd have liked to read languages. But of course it had to be Greats. Anyway I picked up German when I was a kid. My old man used to take us youth-hostelling in the Black Forest. He had a theory about pinewoods and the health-giving qualities of ozone.'

Odd that he made no reference to politics, perhaps they were subsumed under 'bohemian'. Perhaps it was a term that also extended to his marriage to Agnes Moir, buried as securely in his memory as her brother was in some unmarked grave in Spain. But time was slipping by so I got out the tape-recorder and set up the microphone. Colin made a joke about how funny it would be if two professionals between them managed not to get anything on to the tape. Such things had been known to happen. I said not to worry and asked him to say a few words just for level. What he came out with was a couple of verses in the dialect of our part of the world. *'It's dowie at the hint o' hairst? At the wa-gang o' the swallow'* and challenged me to identify the quotation. 'Violet Jacob,' I said, 'pen-name for Violet Erskine of Dun, poet and novelist. 'Pay the gentleman, Barney!' he cracked and explained she had been some sort of relation on his mother's side. We played our little exchange back, joke and all, then I said:

This is tape one of an interview on 23 April 1964 with Colin Elphinstone.

— Mr Elphinstone, may I ask you — is it true the story about you and Janet Munro?

— Good God, what story?

140

— She lived with her father up at Usan, you remember. The story went that you got a ladder one night and climbed through her bedroom window and into her bed.

— No such luck. Although, come to think of it, we did lose our virginities together. In a barn as I remember. I wonder what became of her.

— I saw her on a train once, during the war. You'll be pleased to know she confirmed your version.

— Did she really! She was a smashing lass. I say — this isn't for quotation or reproduction, is it?

— Don't worry, I was just making sure we were actually getting something on the tape. I'm going to wipe that tender memory from the record.

We both laughed. Did I detect, I wondered, a quaver of nervousness in his mirth? Had it perhaps occurred to him that, if I had a memory long enough to recall Janet Munro, I might also cause other things to resurface long repressed beneath the ice-cap of forgetting: if Janet Munro then why not also Agnes Moir? or for that matter, that other Colin, his son, who — so Sue claimed to know — ran a gas-station in Calgary, Alberta, was married with two children and a bit of a drunk.

Then the interview started in earnest to the slight whisper of the spools. Where to begin but at the beginning, with his entry into politics. After all, I put it to him, he could hardly claim to have been a victim of class or economic exploitation. He wasn't underprivileged, and in his origins was even less close to the working class than myself. Could he explain his conversion to Communism? What he produced in reply was a predictable story, with Brian Napier cast as a red-tied Mephisto, founder member of the Oxford October Club, organiser of showings of Russian films, assiduous courtier on the fringe of left-wing literary coteries. The home base, so to speak, was Oxford where politics had less to do with the Morris car-workers than with ploys like playing the *Internationale* — recorded by the Red Army Choir naturally — on a May

141

morning as the madrigals began to sound reedily over the water. But the real scene was London with its marches and rallies, Unity Theatre pantos and a revue — *Love on the Dole*. He could still remember the theme song, which he half sang, half whistled into the microphone. '*Love on the dole/That's a luxury we can't afford/For they don't approve of love on the dole/On the Unemployed Assistance Board.*' He stopped singing and signalled to me to turn off the recorder. Didn't I think there was a programme idea there somewhere? A revival — not in the studio but in that theatre in Stratford East? Then there had been those extraordinary *Living Newspaper* productions with real London busmen playing out the story of their strike, the sort of thing people raved about when they read accounts of them in the Weimar Republic. But of course it wasn't worth while even putting the idea up to any of the television bosses. Nobody was going to look at it. They'd dismiss it with some sophistical doubt about its relevance to the present day. But that was a digression for which he apologized.

When we started up again I suggested that he must have had some more serious and perhaps more compelling reasons for joining the Communist Party — did he mind if I spelt out his allegiance? — than undergrad high spirits. That set him off — with the curious passion that affected him from time to time and now caused the wavering needle of the recorder to leap, so that I had to fiddle to restore the balance — about the anger and shame he had felt in the thirties at belonging to a society that produced three million unemployed, or whatever the exact figure was. It simply hadn't been possible to be even minimally conscious of one's surroundings and not be aware of want and social injustice and of the indifference the ruling class showed to it. Then there was the rise of Fascism and the threat of war. I remarked that there had always seemed to me to be a contradiction between his pacifism — ostentatiously wearing a white poppy on Armistice Day — and his support for the war in Spain. Not to mention the way he had happily gone off to fight Hitler. Not happily, he corrected me; in any case he had not really been a pacifist, merely anti-war and particularly anti imperialist wars. And he had always felt that the Second World War was first and foremost an anti-Fascist war, which was why he had not been a conscientious objector and why he had parted company with the Party, which hadn't really come to its senses until Hitler invaded the Soviet Union. In that case why, I wondered, hadn't he gone to Spain?

— I wanted to but the Party line was that too many intellectuals were getting themselves killed there and this was an intolerable loss.

— Whereas miners were expendable? Like Willie Moir.

— Like Willie Moir.

— Can we talk about his sister, Agnes? Aggie, they called her.

The howling of the wolves intruded into the silence in which he considered my question.

—If you don't mind I think we'll skip that. It's too long ago, too complicated and too painful. And you're not my shrink.

'Well,' Sue commented when I played this exchange back to her, 'you're not, are you?'

'Not what?'

'His shrink, of course, He pays a lady in Hampstead a lot of money to talk about such things.'

'I still think it's rich — very rich,' as I pressed the fast forward.

I said could we discuss something else then. What about the intellectual appeal of Marxism? It was with evident relief that he followed my lead and began to talk about the excitement of reading his first Marxist texts and how — not that he could claim to be a Marxist scholar — there were certain basic assumptions that made sense to him right away, indeed had allowed him for the first time to sort out in his mind much of the conglomerate of facts, dates, names, which had been the staple of his education. Such as? Such as the determining role of economics — in the last analysis, of course — such as the saying that being determines consciousness and not consciousness being. All this had been immensely stimulating and had provided him with a mental framework that had been a great help in his work as an art historian — which was, he supposed, his true métier rather than this dubious business of appearing on the box and making documentaries. Working in Grub Street, as I called it, didn't I? What did I mean, was that all? What more did I want? Unless it was what you might call the utopian side of Marxism: the brotherhood of man, the vision of a communist society. From each according to his abilities, to each according to his needs — wasn't that the formulation? I pointed out that he hadn't even mentioned revolution, which I seemed to remember figured largely on the Communist calendar. He countered, saying that like a lot of other people he had imagined that if we won the war, then there would be an immense social upheaval in any case which would amount to some sort of revolution — the continuation of the extraordinary changes in social attitudes which had come about during the war: many of them positive and just, like rationing, citizen's restaurants, clinics in factories, that sort of thing. The beginning of a new age and the attempt to build a new kind of society. Instead of which we got the Welfare State. Was he complaining? No, he wasn't — it was a big improvement but it wasn't a revolution, which he was increasingly convinced was a rare historical event. He didn't expect to see one in his lifetime. Not in Europe at least.

The tape ran out and whipped round the spool.
    'How was that? Is it any good? I mean — is it what you want? — or expected?'
    'Interesting.'
    'But does it make sense to you?'
    'I think so. How are you fixed for time?'
    'I'm yours till eight. Then I have an immensely boring colloquium, I think they call it, at the Royal College of Art. It will no doubt end up as a boozy evening in the Senior Common Room with a lot of mediocre painters, but with excellent

wine. Nothing common there, dear boy.'

'Then I think we should talk about Cairo.'

'What about Cairo?'

Once again I imagined I detected a trace of nervousness.

'Do you remember the Librairie Internationale?'

'Of course, the best bookshop in town. Run by a chap called Raoul. Spectacles. A bit weedy. Always wore shorts and sandals. A kind of Gandhi figure, I always thought. Jewish but educated *chez les pères*.'

'Rumoured to be a founder member of the Egyptian Communist Party. Has quite a history. Now lives in Rome, having been expelled from France for being mixed up in the Algerian resistance.'

'That sounds to his credit.'

'Suspected — if you can trust the French and Italian press —'

'Can you?'

'Of being involved in a vast international terrorist network.'

'I'd like to know where they dredged this up from. I think all accusations like that are to be taken with a pinch of salt. Unless there is very strong, untainted evidence.'

'But you had no idea?'

'Well, maybe a suspicion — but like most people I was really interested in that amazing bunch of girls that worked there. As a matter of fact I had one of these brief wartime romances with one of them.'

'Yvette.'

'How clever of you to remember.'

With whom, damn him, he danced off that hot evening to the tune of *Deep is the Night* so that she never came back to me.

'I say — that thing's not running, is it?'

I reassured him.

'Do you know what she said the first time we made love?'

'Tell me.'

'Tiens! Tu n'es pas juif!'

'My God,' exclaimed Sue when I related the episode to her, 'I thought he only told that story to his girl friends.'

I set the spools turning and the little needle peaked to his laughter and asked — seriously though — whether he had really no idea what was going on politically at the bookshop.

Well, yes, he had wondered once. There had been this curious incident during the mutiny of the Greek brigade in the Middle East, who objected — very reasonably — to having royalist and other right-wing officers imposed on them. He had dropped into Raoul's flat to see if Yvette was there and found a guy called Georges, who was in civvies. He might have been anything — Egyptian, Greek, Lebanese. Just before Colin decided to leave there was a phone call following which Raoul asked would he mind going down in the lift with Georges and walking along the street a bit with him. He didn't explain why, although it was pretty obvious when they got out of the lift and there was a truckful of military police at the entrance to the block with a sergeant who — impressed no doubt by Colin's regimentals, his rank and his medal ribbons — threw him a very smart salute as they walked off. A couple of minutes later Georges vanished up a side street. And that was that.

— And you never asked Raoul what it was all about?
— It would have been — what shall I say? — tactless.
— But looking back you must have had an inkling.
— Of course I had an inkling.
— Meaning that he was probably one of the Greek mutineers?'
— Right.
— And that didn't bother you?
— No, because I felt then — and still feel now — that the Greek troops were in the right.
— But it could have got you into big trouble.
— It was something I did — like that. Instinctively. I had no hesitations, no qualms, no regrets.
— Some people might say you were irresponsible.
— You remember that great Scottish saying: They say —

146

What they say let them say.

— A bit haughty, don't you think?

— All I know is — to put it in Marxist terms — that in this world any situation is riddled with contradictions. This was one of them.

— Does that mean there were others?

— Naturally. Different though.

He paused and thought for a moment. Outside the noise of the traffic was like waves breaking on a distant reef.

— You know I was commissioned into my father's old regiment. First Battalion and all that. Joined it in fact just in time for the last big scrap against the Italians in Eritrea. In the mountains, a placed called Keren. They fought well there. Admittedly in strong positions — an escarpment rising up to something like seven thousand feet — no way round it and only one road through it. Which had to be forced. But what a bloody awful country to fight in. Like the Alps without the snow. Nothing but rocks and boulders and scree. Thorn scrub and prickly pear. Full of baboons too. They used to blow themselves up by collecting those funny little red hand-grenades the Eyties had, which had a habit of not going off. Not at first at least. And they dug up the dead. Anyway we ended up in Asmara, passing the time till someone somewhere decided where to send us next. Doing ridiculous parade-ground drills and manoeuvres. Forming squares — to repel cavalry, don't you know. And — you won't believe this — practising Highland dancing to the pipes before breakfast. Great training for dealing with Rommel's Africa Corps tanks, what! Meantime the night-clubs of Asmara flourished. The girls were friendly. We got drunk in their company. We danced with them. Some people managed to go to bed with them. They had a marvellous musky smell. The different battalions had favourite night-spots. Our adjutant led a raid on an establishment which an English county battalion claimed as its preserve. We kidnapped the leading dancer and carted her off to our own place. She was one of the most beautiful women I have ever seen. Tall and very slim. I remember our

147

brigade-major dancing on a table to celebrate and falling off. There was a well-appointed officers' brothel to which the authorities turned a blind eye. Some people went there to play bridge. There was a regular school. Others went up stairs past the madam and the half-crippled, spinsterish woman who sat at the receipt of custom at a sort of turnstile. The girls were all Italian and wanted to know when they would be going home to *la bell'Italia*. If you went round next morning there was the madam serving *zabaglione* as a pick-me-up. You needed something for the long marches we did through the country-side. What the regulars, who had had practice at this sort of thing on the North West Frontier, called 'showing the flag'. Children herding goats on the bare hillsides watched us march past with the pipes playing and the Jocks cursing the heat and the altitude. A handful of peasants came down from their huddled hill-top villages to inspect us. The women — they were tall with tight fuzzy hair — had a marvellous bearing. The MO put it about, however, that all native women were poxed up to the gills. The children who came begging round the cantonment where we were quartered were ragged and had some disease of the eyes. It caused a constant discharge and the flies clustered on it in black rings. The regular officers — they had spent twenty years or so in India — felt completely at home. They went off to shoot sand grouse or lie in wait for wild pig at drinking-holes. But they usually got tight as they waited and missed them. All they brought back once was a wretched green parrot someone had taken a pot-shot at. Then one day we got orders to carry out a search on some village. There was a theory that the natives had got hold of abandoned Italian arms and might be up to something — what wasn't clear — and we had to look for the stuff. So just before dawn we got out of our transport a mile short of a hill-top village and took up positions surrounding it with our light machine-guns covering the obvious escape routes. I watched the dim phosphorescence of my watch-hands and as they came to five fired a flare. It was first light. As the flare drooped over the rooftops we went in. My platoon sergeant, a regular with

God knows how many years service in India — not a bad man, just totally institutionalised, as the sociologists say, and contemptuous of all wogs — pushed open the door of a hut and we barged in. It was low-roofed and smelt of wood-smoke and human bodies, which stirred and rose in the half-light. Men, women with babies, young girls, children. They were very frightened. An old man came forward and said something in a sort of broken Italian mixed with Arabic. No one paid any attention to him. I told the sergeant and six men to search the place, carefully. It ran back into the rock of the hillside and was more a cave-dwelling than a hut. No rooms, just compartments divided off with wood and bits of canvas and sacking. There were a few pots and pans by the stone hearth with its cold ashes. There was an old alarm clock and an acetylene lamp hanging from a hook in the ceiling. There were one or two chests and some wooden-frame string beds. Greyish clothes lay about in ragged heaps. But there were no arms. I said okay, that was it, and we walked out into the cold thin air of the high plateau. The old man came to the door to watch our withdrawal. He was very calm. I wished I could say something — apologize in some way — explain that this was one of the idiocies of colonialism and war. Behind him a woman with a child on her hip looked steadily at me with unmistakable hatred. We clambered into our trucks and drove back for breakfast. Over his bacon and eggs the CO recalled village searches on the Frontier. It was agreed that this one had been a bit of a non-event but good training for the Jocks. Kept them on their toes. Otherwise they'd get terribly slack and even more poxed up than they were already. God knows where they got it. Native women down in the bazaar, he imagined. I sat and listened. I had done my duty as a servant of the King-Emperor and I didn't like the thought. In fact it made me want to puke.

There was a silence. I used it to change the tape. Colin poured himself another whisky. As I fiddled with the machine I pondered the warmth of feeling with which he had spoken of

149

the anonymous cave-dwellers of Eritrea compared with his treatment of Agnes Moir, buried in the deep freeze, the morgue of his memory.

This is tape two of an interview with Colin Elphinstone on 23 April 1964.

— Just for the record can we get you back from Eritrea and into Yugoslavia?

— Right. Eventually we came back to the desert. I was terribly lucky and managed to wangle an attachment to the Long Range Desert Group. Pretty boring most of the time, actually, except that you were some hundreds of miles behind the enemy lines, lying up there in the camel thorn in that appalling heat and counting the traffic on the coast road to the front. Trucks. Tank conveyors. Lorry-loads of troops. Did you know there was a travelling brothel — Italian, of course — that went up once a week? Other ranks, for the use of, I expect. We made a point of including it in our returns. Then I came back to Cairo for a spell. Kicking my heels in Head-quarters. But of course you were there and know all about that. Then I had a piece of real luck. I ran into a chap I had known at Oxford, met him at the Gerzira races, actually. He was in the Special Operations Executive, and he managed to get me on to the mission to Tito.

— Having meantime married Diana Carter Pomfret.

— Yes, dear Diana. It was very good while it lasted and mind you, it lasted a fair time. Nine years to be exact. And then, as they say, we simply grew apart.

Diana, too, buried in the ice of his memory. An ice-maiden herself, perhaps she didn't mind.

— Then there was Yugoslavia.
— Then, as you say, there was Yugoslavia.
— I liked your book.
— Thank you.
— What did Tom Pressman think of it?
— Tom Pressman. Radio operator. A marvellous guy.

150

— You knew him pretty well, I take it?

— It's difficult not to when you've tramped across most of Montenegro with someone. With his transmitting gear and his mule. Damnably stubborn it was too.

— I had an idea you knew him before that. In London.

— One knew a lot of people in London — before the war.

— But you met up again in Cairo.

— That was extraordinary. There I was sitting waiting for Diana in some café when I saw this sergeant at the next table reading Flaubert's *Education Sentimentale*, so we got chatting and discovered he'd been up at Oxford with some people I knew who had been very involved in Spain. So it was on the cards we'd met. An amazing chap. A grammar-school boy from the East End. A wonderful linguist.

— And a hard-line Stalinist.

— Believe me, at the time it didn't seem very important.

— But you saw eye to eye on things.

— Like that the war had to be won. That Tito, if he actually existed — which some people doubted — might be a big help in that direction.

— In retrospect — judging by that book he wrote — Pressman didn't have too good an opinion of Tito. Not subservient enough to Stalin.

— I'm afraid we rather lost touch, you know how it is.

— To come back to Cairo, there's a theory around that things like that extraordinary Soldiers' Parliament, which people like our friend Pressman organized there, played a big part in preparing the ground for the Labour victory in 1945.

— I've always thought it was the armed forces vote that put paid to Churchill. Ironical, isn't it? But then they hadn't been exposed to quite the same extent to all that oratory on the BBC and in the House. I think the ordinary squaddie remembered the dole and the means test, the hunger marches and simply didn't want to come home to more of the same sort of thing. And they were fed up to the back teeth — quite rightly in my opinion — with the sheer incompetence of a

151

lot of the regular officers from — what shall I call them? — the ruling classes? Or am I showing a tiny cloven hoof? People like my company commander, jolly brave and all that but thick and with not the faintest idea how to fight a modern war. All that galloping to and fro across North Africa. What they used to call the Western Desert Stakes. They really had an amazing knack for lapses of taste. You know what they called the attack that finished off my battalion in Normandy? Operation Goodwood — because that day they should really have been at the races. 26th June 1944, that was.

— Some people might say —

— That I come out of the same top drawer. All right, even if it's a bit of an exaggeration. But remember my father was a Liberal before the First World War, when the Liberals were still a radical party. And when the Spanish Civil War came there he was, stumping the country at seventy in support of the Republic.

— But as we know you didn't go there.

— I suppose I felt that World War Two, in spite of massive contradictions, was a continuation of the same fight. So, in a sense, I didn't miss out.

— Tell me, did you know about Ultra?

— I was never on the list.

— Not like Diana.

— Right. If you were on the list that was the end of going on ops. Of course I had an inkling.

— From Diana?

— You must be joking. She was very secure.

— How then?

— From odd remarks people made in GHQ. I bet you guessed too.

— If you had felt it would have helped to win the war if the Russians had knowledge of Ultra, would you have slipped them the word?

— Listen, the only Russian I saw until the end of the war was a lonely character in baggy trousers looking into a shop-window in Cairo.

152

— And today?

— I can't imagine that I know anything of the slightest interest to the Soviet Authorities.

— What about the East Germans?

— You know what politicians say on the box when they're asked that sort of question.

— I know. So it should be — Mr Elphinstone, thank you very much and now back to the Panorama studio. But you do know something of interest to them. You know there's a tunnel being dug under the Berlin Wall.

— So do a lot of people. So do you.

— What about Schneider?

— What about Schneider?

— Does he know?

— Why should he?

— Well, you were pretty thick with him. At the Congress, I mean. Tête-à-têtes by the lake. Rides in official cars.

There was a pause in which he marshalled his thoughts. Decided how to react.

— Poor old Schneider. He has problems. Slight difficulties with the authorities. Nothing terrible. Annoyances as much as anything else, really. He wanted to talk to someone. Why not me? Or are you suggesting . . . ?

— I was just asking.

— Then I think I'll give the standard reply. I'm sorry, but I don't answer hypothetical questions.

We both laughed a little nervously. I turned off the recording gear. Darkness had fallen. The Post Office Tower rose from the glow of the city. 'Like a giant vibrator,' said Colin, catching the direction of my glance. 'I forgot who called it that, but I like it. Have another before you go.' I refused because I was supposed to be cutting down and was conscious that I had drunk too much already that evening, and had been trapped into softness and so had lost the game we had been playing. 'No? Then I must be off to this boring colloquium.' Hand on shoulder in a gesture that might have been one of friendship or again might have been one of dismissal and was probably a bit of both, he guided me to the door. On the threshold he accepted my thanks in a perfunctory way. He felt he'd rambled on a bit. No, he didn't think there was much point in another session. In any case he was probably going to be out of the country for a while. 'Give my love to Sue when next you see her. A marvellous lass. Such a pity she threw things up and went into publishing. Well, goodbye, old chap. Nice to talk about Yvette and all that. *Les neiges d'antan.* I hope it helps. With the book I mean.'

The Times: 23 October 1964

BERLIN WALL TUNNEL DISCOVERED
The East German authorities today announced that an attempt by three men and a woman to escape from East Berlin by means of a tunnel under the Berlin Wall has been foiled. According to an official announcement two men were arrested. The woman and one man were killed during an exchange of shots. The East German authorities claim that the tunnel was planned by the CIA in collaboration with an American television network. The tunnel originates, they claim, in the American sector. The American authorities in Berlin said that they had no comment to make on the story. None of the American networks would confirm their participation in the escape attempt. It is believed that television crews had been standing by to film the escapers as they emerged into the West.

The Sunday Record: 26 October 1964

TRAGEDY IN BERLIN
Who betrayed the freedom dash?
Bill Gilchrist reports:
All denials apart it is clear that there was an attempt to engineer not one but a series of escapes by means of a tunnel under the Berlin Wall, which has already claimed so many lives.

There is no doubt in my mind that one of the main American television networks was deeply involved and indeed probably funded the project in return for exclusive coverage of the fugitives making their break to freedom from the repression of the East German state.

Through contacts in West Berlin I was able to visit the cellar — its location is still a closely guarded secret — where the Western end of the tunnel began. These exclusive pictures show that this was one of the best organized and best planned attempts to open a doorway to freedom. Through it groups of brave men and women from the so-called Democratic Republic of East Germany might have found their way to a new life.

My sources tell me that security was very tight on the whole operation. Only a handful of people — American and German — were in the know. Yet someone tipped off the dreaded Stasis, the state security police on the other side of the grim frontier that runs across the face of this great city.

As a consequence of someone's treachery the Wall has claimed two more victims. No doubt the American and West German authorities will be following up any clues as to the identity of the person who so shamefully betrayed these courageous fugitives from the East.

I shall be reporting next week on developments in a special article on Berlin, city of spies and secret agents.

'Well,' said Malcolm. That's quite a story Mr Gilchrist's come up with. Did you see the telly last night? They showed the tunnel. You should have seen it. Electric light. A telephone. Right down in a basement. D'you think he knew — Mr Gilchrist? I thought he was just away doing a wee bit of fishing again. But it looks as if he was there or thereabout.' I said I expected so and finished drinking. Grace was gracious when I said goodnight. Her horse had come in at five to one in the two thirty at Plumpton. In Oxford Street there was a bluster of wind and rain. The pavements were empty. The maws of the tube had swallowed the stream of secretaries,

155

clerks, shop-girls. Under the earth they were borne — successful tunnellers — to freedom in bed-sits, in semis in the far suburbs, in the terraced houses of forgotten villages where the lavender fields had once spread. *Sutton for mutton/Carshalton for beef/Croydon for a pretty girl/And Mitcham for a thief.*

On my desk the usual angry note from Liz. Ring Mr Gilchrist and a number. So he was back, writing that special report of his no doubt. Maybe that was why he hadn't come to Grace's. It was a woman who answered. A curious accent. She handed me to Mr Gilchrist, who said could I come to his place. Malcolm was right, it was in Shepherd's Market where there must have been an attempt by the police to clean the place up — no doubt for the benefit of the American tourists — because only half-open doors with illuminated bell-pushes invited the few punters who roamed the mews lanes like dogs on the scent of a bitch on heat. The address was in a modern block of flats grafted on to the old village houses. Gilchrist himself came to the entryphone and bade me find a number on the second floor where he was already waiting at the open door. With a 'Come away ben' he led me through a hall hung with sporting prints, past an immense stuffed, hook-jawed salmon — caught by Gilchrist? bought at an auction? — and into a room furnished with the impersonality of a motel lounge. Low tables, large easy chairs. Pictures on the wall that looked as if they had been bought off the railings at Hyde Park on a Sunday morning. 'That was good o' ye to come,' he said. 'I thought maybe it would be a wee bit more private here than at Grace's. She and that Malcolm, they've ears like saucers, the pair of them.' As he began the ritual of lighting a cigarette — tapping it on his cigarette-case, producing the lighter with a flourish and a shooting of the cuffs — a door opened and a tall, striking black girl came in. Her skin had a slightly ruddy colouring; her mouth was full and glistening with lipstick; her whole body was compact, firm, strong. She said nothing but came to lean over the back of Gilchrist's chair. 'This is Gloria,' he said. She looked at me with a total lack of interest and said: 'Hi!' 'Gloria, give Mr Melville a drink. He likes malt.' Her duties performed, she returned to her post behind his chair. 'Slainte,' said Gilchrist and raised his glass. 'Gloria, hen, Mr Melville and I have something to discuss.' She gave a glistening pout and left the room silently with a roll of the hips. Gilchrist made no attempt to explain her presence or function and I did not ask. 'Well,' he began. 'I wanted to thank you for the wee prezzy.' He nodded towards a side-table where for the first time I noticed the two small square cardboard boxes which must contain the tapes. 'Very interesting. But I'm not sure what I'm supposed to do with them. Or what you want out of it.' He inclined his fox's face towards mine and smiled. 'Of course, there could be the odd shilling in it for you — if you were prepared to sell the rights outright to the paper and didn't mind the end of a beautiful friendship. I've had a word with the editor and he's said I can talk terms. Of course we'd have to take counsel's advice before using any of the material. Mind you, it has to be said that it's all very circumstantial. All right, there's this stuff about the Communist Party and the gentleman's first marriage and a couple of other indiscretions, very interesting but background stuff mostly. It's when we get down to Schneider and the tunnel that it looks a wee bit thin. Still it's worth a whirl.' He paused and considered the ash at the end of his cigarette, then tapped it accurately into an ash-tray. 'I wonder though — have you had a word with your friends? And what did they say about it?'

Nisbett squinted through the cigarette smoke, cackling like a hen, and said that it was all very interesting but wasn't I perhaps giving a little too much weight to my evidence? After all, they might indeed have been talking about Mr Schneider's troubles with the authorities rather than about the tunnel, which in his view was an idiotic and typically transatlantic idea anyway. But no doubt our American friends would be interested. It really was more their ball than ours, he couldn't help feeling. And then Weston, apparently bored and dismissive, as if I were a child bringing home some ridiculous fantasy.

'Don't tell me,' said Gilchrist. 'They look after their own. And they don't learn. Now if it was some poor bugger who didn't go to the right school, didn't have the right accent and know the right people, the boys in the raincoats would be calling to have a little chat. But not with Master Elphinstone, the great left-winger who treats people like me like shit and thinks he can play about politically and get away with it. Well this time we'll see.'

For a couple of hours we sat and drank. Gilchrist spoke. Of his youth in the back courts of Dundee, of the family shop with the hot scent of rolls and butteries and his father, white-faced, girt with a white towel and constantly powdered with flour, who would take the back of his hand to the boy's face at the slightest misdemeanour and how Gilchrist had realized that there was one avenue of escape open to him — through schooling. How without anyone to put in a good word for him he had got into the newspaper business and pulled himself up by sheer effort when other people who had been to the right schools and had the right accent went into the so-called quality papers or into the BBC or television — like my friend — without qualifications, without experience, never having had to do the leg-work, the foot-in-the-door stuff, the weddings, the funerals, the murders and the suicides. The sort of thing they despised people like him for. He'd like to see one of them dictate a story to a copy-taker at one in the morning, with a dead man lying with his throat cut in the council house behind the phone booth, and the widow having a fit and the bairns howling at her skirts. And they were the people who called themselves socialists and talked about the working class. What they knew about the working class could go on the back of a postage stamp. But that was the way it was, Jock, except that now and again one of these toffee-nosed bastards put a foot wrong. Which was where they could get

158

their come-uppance and he'd be happy to help to arrange it. At some point Gloria came in with a glass of whisky in her hand and took up position behind his chair. He raised his hand with a gesture of affection and touched her cheek. I said I'd better be getting back. Gloria watched me go with an indifferent smile. Gilchrist was fairly tight. At the door he grasped my hand warmly and bade me 'guid nicht' and said something about being in touch over you know what. When I came out into the street the rain had stopped. On my way out into Curzon Street, where the bulk of Nisbett's office block rose darkly, a tall girl in thigh-length leather boots and a remarkably short skirt brushed past me and said 'Hello, dearie,' but I shook my head and walked off towards the tube.

Why did no one but Gilchrist begin to understand? Why did the logic of the argument escape them? A logic so clear and obvious that it required no empirical proof: no bugged conversations, no intercepts, no evidence written or spoken. Merely some knowledge of human nature in general and of a man like Colin Elphinstone in particular. There was no point in rehearsing the argument to Sue who in these matters was not so much sceptical as impervious to reason — an attitude that stemmed less from any rigorous examination of the evidence than from a quirk that made her, despite hurts and wounds grown over but ready to bleed at a touch, still quick to protect Colin. But why did professionals like Nisbett and Weston not see the clear line that led through Schneider from Hamburg to London to East Germany to Berlin and on to that lakeside in Yugoslavia where the indiscretion — which was no doubt how Colin would describe it — had taken place, inspired by run-of-the-mill anti-Americanism touched off, more than likely, by that conversation with Greenspan. A protest, he would no doubt argue, against the combination of commercialism and politics, the exploitation of hopes and aspirations for gain; as if people in that situation could afford to be nice about who sponsored their break-out or could

159

afford to play things according to some book of rules which only Master Elphinstone knew. So that morally he was in the clear. All he had done was to cry Foul. It was not his fault if the result was a couple of deaths and a few arrests.

Which were more or less the arguments I put forward to the couple of visitors in raincoats who called at the *dépendance* about a week later; which I took as a heartening sign that some one — Nisbett? Weston? — had begun to see the light. They were courteous and non-committal. Mr Halcro took a fancy to one of them and tried to jump up onto his lap but was repelled. Maybe it was against the rules to pay attention to pets when on duty.

Some time after they called, there came a phone call from Sue — from her office obviously — demanding to know what the hell I had been up to now and requiring me to come over that evening since there were some things she preferred not to discuss on the phone. I presumed it was something to do with Colin but I could hardly believe that she too had been 'seen', as Nisbett would say. At about seven I reluctantly went out into the damp of the evening. The leaves glistened under foot on the pavements. On the Heath there were the usual steamed-up cars in the parking place; inside them vague shapes manoeuvred in the give and take of sexual advantage. There was a bank of mist over the ponds where the ducks slept on the bank, head under wing, and, waking, slithered to the water when a dog arrived noisily, heedless of its master calling from the other side of the water. I lingered a little by the water's edge where old feathers, pieces of paper and a used French letter bobbed at the margin. I still had in my pocket — unopened — the letter from Gilchrist's paper, which had arrived a couple of days before and which must contain a proposition or even the cheque itself. It was as if, by refusing to open it, I could delay the consummation of my betrayal. Had Colin, I wondered, also been visited — or were they still evaluating the evidence? deciding whether to reveal their hand? I took the envelope from my inside jacket pocket — it had become slightly crumpled — and examined it under a lamp-post where the light filtered weakly through the damp air. It told me nothing new: the date of posting, the fact that it was from the paper. With my finger I tried to make the transparent window reveal more than my address; but it was very secure. A young man, tall and blond, with a slight accent that might have been South African, came walking along the footpath, stopped, made some remark about the weather and wondered if I'd like to come round to his place, which was just across the Heath. When I said I wasn't interested he walked off smartly. I waited till he was out of sight. Then I shredded the envelope, which was tough at first but gradually gave and tore. I was careful not to look at the contents, at their colour or consistency, but worked persistently at their destruction. When the pieces were small enough I went down and sowed them along the dark water. That done I set off quickly to Sue's flat.

She let me in without a word. Penelope was more welcoming but at a word from her mistress slunk off into the kitchen. Well, what was it all about? I asked. And why all the secrecy? Was she really suggesting that her office phone was tapped? She did not sit down but walked to and fro. Her face was very pale with a tiny hectic spot on her high cheek-bones. Not a good sign. She turned the question back on me, deploying one of the gambits we had developed and perfected. 'What's it all about? It's about the fact that I had a phone call from Colin after all these years. Asking whether he could come round. Do you know the last thing I heard from him? A note — handwritten — saying: Thank you for the gift of sensuality. Can you beat it? That was when he dumped me.' She stopped began to pace the room again. 'I knew from his voice,' she went on at least, 'he was in a terrible state. Probably drunk. So he comes round. Slumming, you might say. I gave him a big whisky and we talked. It seems he's had a journalist on his tail for days, a man called Gilchrist from one of the Sundays. Very well genned up. Accusing him of all kinds of things. Threatening to expose him.' 'What sort of things?' I asked. 'Come on,' she retorted. 'You know.' 'Such as —' 'Such as that he was a security risk. Such as that he was an undercover member of the CP. Such as that he had acted as a courier. Such as that he had betrayed some tunnel in West Berlin to the East German authorities.' 'So what were you supposed to do about it?' She looked at me intently. 'What do you think I was supposed to do? Comfort him — the way I used to comfort him when we worked together. If a day's filming went badly. If the labs messed up a print. If a can of film got lost, if he was stuck on an edit or some executive didn't like his latest programme suggestion. If he lost his nerve — for he does lose it, you know, with nightmares and cold sweats, the lot. He wanted to go to bed with good old Sue — not necessarily to screw, you understand. Just to be held and cuddled and made better. So that he wouldn't be frightened any more of falling into a pit of despair. Just like the good old days!' 'And did you oblige?' I asked out of curiosity. 'That's none of your business,' she said. 'I'm telling you so that you know what sort of state he's in. And it's your bloody fault.' 'Did he say it was?' He was, she explained, too bloody naïve — too arrogant or too nice, depending on how you looked at it — too certain that people are basically decent (which was what his politics had always really been about), too much of an idiot, to believe that some-one who was a friend of his could sell him down the river. 'Have you?' she asked sharply. 'What?' 'Sold him down the river.' I thought of the cheque cast in shreds upon the waters and said: 'Certainly not!' 'But you've done something. I know you, I know you absolutely, through and through. It has all the signs. John Melville, his mark. This Gilchrist — he's that boozy hack I've heard you talk about. One of Grace's regulars. Another fucking Scotsman.' I shrugged and said if Gilchrist had theories he had plenty of other sources to get them from. Why didn't she just relax. Lie down. Go to bed. Take some-thing for her migraine. We could talk about it another time when she felt better. As I spoke she suddenly rushed out. I

162

could hear her retching her guts up in the loo. When she came back her face was an odd yellow colour. 'Go on,' I said, 'Go to bed. I'll get you a hotwater bottle. Take one of your pills and tomorrow you'll feel better.' She was suddenly obedient. When I left she was asleep with Penelope curled up beside her bed. I was almost tempted to get in beside her and comfort her the way she herself had had to be comforted in the early days when we were first together and the wounds Colin had dealt her were still fresh; but that was a long time ago. Instead I walked slowly home through the cold damp night. At least there was no call from Colin on my answering-machine. I poured a big whisky, drank it, had another, fed Mr Halcro and went to bed.

PART III

My secretary, Liz, laid the package on my desk so gingerly that it might have been a letter-bomb. A cardboard package fastened with white camera-tape and addressed in a woman's hand. A clump of Greek stamps. No sender's name. The postmark was blurred and indecipherable. Inside the magnetic tape was carefully wound on the spool and the end neatly secured. We had no tape-machine in the office. I did not possess one of my own. However before the office closed I had negotiated the loan of one on a strictly unofficial basis from a talks producer in Bush House for whom I did occasional pieces — interviews with visiting trade unionists and social democrat politicians, actuality pieces for magazine programmes. The stock-in-trade of the radio hack. Back at the *dépendance* I set the stove blazing, poured myself a drink and put the spool in the machine. There was a slight background noise — a door banging, distant voices, a car starting up — then after a pause, as if the speaker were gathering his resolution, he began.

This is tape three of an interview with Colin Elphinstone. Well, not so much an interview, more a monologue. I am taping this in my bedroom in a hotel in Ag. Nic., which is what my camera crew call Agios Nicolaos — Saint Nicholas, to you — old Santa Claus himself, who has given his name — very appositely, you may think — to a holiday resort in Crete, packed, dear boy, with all the goodies your average tourist has come to expect in the way of souvenirs, chips, and discos. Although this being the off-season — who was the thirties poet — can it have been Ashburton? — who said August is for the people? — the place is relatively quiet and the German

167

tourists are not yet being decanted on to the tarmac at Heraklion, which remembers another invasion when the German airborne troops came floating in. I say invasion though what right — if you think about it — you or I or anybody else has to be patronizing about package tours beats me. Anyway the crew have gone off with dear Eva, my new PA, with whom — let me reassure you — I am not repeat not sleeping, although she is attractive, blonde, twenty-five-ish, recently widowed — her husband crashed in a light plane trying to get news-film of a couple of climbers stuck on the north face of the Eiger — and therefore no doubt in need of comforting and not that I don't think it mightn't perhaps be pleasant. Simply that it would just be too damned complicated and life is complicated enough already. Besides, it may be the ageing process but I am beginning to agree with poor Semyonov — you remember Semyonov with his *Flowers of Ice* — I picked it up the other day and came across an extraordinary piece where he talks about the sadness of men who collect women — and women who collect men — the way other people collect stamps or match-boxes. It makes you think, if I may coin a phrase. And makes me wonder how you are fixed these days. Not with Sue any more I gather. Good old Sue — I saw her recently — when I wasn't feeling too good and gave her a tinkle on the spur of the moment. For old times' sake. She really is a brick and loyal to a degree. Why did we have to have that incestuous relationship — you and I? Peer-group rivalry, I think they call it, or were you just sorry for her because I suppose I was a bit of a shit dumping her like that, but it really didn't work any more for her or me. At all events here I sit in single blessedness while Eva and the crew have gone off to have the nearest thing they can find to a decent English meal, because for a variety of reasons — cultural, social, class — they are sick of souvlaki and Greek salads and find the ouzo, the retsina and the raki disgusting. Whereas I have a bottle of the stuff — the raki, I mean — beside me and find it comforting. Something you as an old soak will understand. Perhaps it is just as well that we are near the end of our assignment and there are really only two more locations to be covered. Difficult ones, though. In the mountains. Tomorrow's Sunday and the crew want a break, which I don't grudge them, they've worked bloody well — so I shall go swanning off by myself on a recce. To the cave where Zeus was born, though I notice from my guidebook that quote the location is disputed by scholars unquote. I like that little bit of academic scruple. Anyway the descent into the cave — and I quote again — is steep and somewhat slippery and the lower depths are chilly. And no doubt — though of course it doesn't say so and this is merely my gloss — exceedingly difficult to light and shoot in. Deities do choose odd birthplaces, don't you think? It can't have been very nice for Zeus' mum, Hera, who was expecting a difficult time in any case because Daddy Chronos had the nasty habit of devouring his children and had already gobbled up five, no less. Which reminds me of that hymn that talks about time like an ever-rolling stream and how it bears all its sons away. I remember we sang it in chapel at prep school one Armistice Day and I was overcome with terror at the thought of death. Did you ever stumble upon the thought of your own mortality like that? But I digress because I am a little tight and inclined perhaps to ramble a little but bear with me and let me press on to remind you that Zeus the Thunderer survived because Rhea presented her hubby with a stone wrapped up in swaddling clothes which he rushed off with like a dog with a bone. He must have been a bit dim, don't you think, old Father Time, to be taken in quite so easily? No doubt he has been ratty ever since. And takes it out on mere mortals. However that may be, by all accounts the road up to the cave is execrable and immensely steep before you come out on to a high plateau above the olive-tree line and I don't entirely trust the brakes of the clapped-out car I've hired. It would be so much nicer, don't you think, if we could fly like the buzzard or maybe it was an eagle I saw yesterday, big and black above the plain, riding the thermals over towards Mount Ida where, let me remind you again, since I am by now an authority on the subject, baby Zeus was safely hidden away and raised by the

169

goat-nymph, Amaltheia. I think we probably saw her this morning under an olive-tree: white, full-uddered, with great flared nostrils, yellow eyes and beautifully curved, tapering horns. Can't you imagine — and don't you at some level envy (because I do) — that lucky baby latching on to these great tits and clinging to the warm, smelly fleece? But back to what we call reality. Mount Ida is our very last location. From which of course you will have gathered that I am doing another of Colin Elphinstone's prestigious documentaries which look so good in the BBC Year Book. No expense spared, well hardly any. About Crete and the Minoan culture, to be called — but you must promise to keep this under your hat and not spill it to the press who, for reasons we shall come to, are taking a great interest in me — but then you're very secure, aren't you? (*A brief bark of a laugh*) I beg your pardon but I think that was rather funny — called, as I was about to say, *The Bull from the Sea*. All those marvellous gold-hilted swords and crystalline vases and the terracotta votive offerings from that very cave I was talking about. Little figurines, some of them rather rude and, as the latter-day puritans say, explicit. Copulating, not to put too fine a point on it. And the tiny beads of gold filigree on the jewellery that looks like the work of some immensely industrious insect. But what a relief in the museums to be able to walk past all those endless cases of dreary brown Greek vases which numb the mind and make your eyes glaze merely to look at them. Of course all this waffle, as you have probably guessed, is — what do they call it in animals? — I know, a diversionary activity to prevent me from coming to the point and asking you, John Melville, old acquaintance, old friend — I can call you an old friend, can't I? — the boy who beat me at golf one summer afternoon long before the war — a question. Which is, to be perfectly clear not to say blunt: What the fuck do you mean by putting that man Gilchrist on to me? ringing me up? demanding an interview or else? threatening me with exposure? So that I have a reporter and a photographer permanently in ambush outside the flat and people ringing poor

170

old Eva up at work and at home wanting to know about my movements, my friends and my love-life — as if she didn't have enough worries of her own — so that to be able to get here and make this film in peace I had to change planes twice and travel under a false name. Calling myself John Melville, which I thought was a nice jape because I'm taking it as proven beyond any reasonable doubt that it was you that started it all. For however diligent Mr Gilchrist may be — and by Jesus he had done his homework — he'd bloody well need to be psychic to know, not that I was at the conference in Zelena Gora — any journalist worth his salt could find that out with a bit of luck — but that Hermann Schneider and I talked together. On a terrace, as I remember, above the lake where you came gumshoeing down after us so that we had to drive off together in an official car. Which was not a very good idea as far as he was concerned. Now I know Mr Gilchrist loathes my guts and has had it in for me for a long time but what I'd like to ask you first of all is what have I ever done to you to make you want to destroy me? Because that is what you seem to want to do. Are you some sort of spook? I've often wondered. Or is it just a kind of envy, a sense of impotence that fills people like you with anger and hate and can — politically speaking — push them in all sorts of directions. To Fascism, to terrorism, to radical lunacies of one kind or another. At least towards some kind of revenge on the destiny that caused you to be born — in terms of class, if the word isn't tabu — between the upper and the nether millstones, which can grind exceeding small. Come to think of it the real difference between us is that I may be a traitor to my class, indulging — remember that old army tag? — in conduct unbecoming to an officer and a gentleman, but you, dear boy, belong to a class that is by its nature treacherous. Why has no one ever written about it, I wonder? So much more interesting than penis envy, don't you think? But then who am I — as I believe I have just said — to play the shrink? However, just for the record let me say now and categorically that I did not repeat not mention the tunnel to Hermann, who was much too concerned about

171

his own position and his problems vis-à-vis the authorities in the GDR to be interested in a tunnel under the Wall. In any case it didn't need me to tell these same authorities that something fishy was going on. I picked it up without too much trouble in a bar in Berlin. Gilchrist picked it up. So why shouldn't the Stasis have got on to it as well? One thing I do know is that it makes me sick to read pieces by Gilchrist talking about martyrs for freedom and democracy. I'd need to know a lot more about the poor sods involved before I said yes and amen to that. If Gilchrist was honest he'd have to admit that they were the victims of a propaganda exercise, pieces in a dangerous game that various people — including the CIA and, who knows, maybe the security forces on the other side — set up on the front line of the Cold War. Which would be a damned sight nearer the truth but not such a good story for Gilchrist and his editor and his disgusting newspaper. Which is more or less, you may remember, what I told that terrible man, Greenspan — by the way, I must tell you a funny story about him — whom I saw the other evening on some programme in full cry defending US policies in Vietnam in the name of freedom and Western democracy. In which connection let me remind you that there's a great tradition of sacrificing other people in the name of democracy and freedom. At the risk of boring you, my old treacherous friend, let me give you an example. Out of pure curiosity I drove out the other evening — alone, I may say, because the crew and dear Eva find such matters incomprehensible and infinitely remote — to a village on the road to Mount Ida. Shall I tell you what happened there? It was flattened by the Germans because the villagers had helped a couple of English agents who had — very daringly — kidnapped a German general. Why did they kidnap him? It's a good question and I'm glad you asked it. I can't believe it affected the course of the war one way or the other. He didn't know much. He wasn't very important. But it was fun, wasn't it? To pick him up, get him out of Crete and back to Cairo. Jolly good show, what? Sounded great on the BBC news. I remember going with Diana when we were —

as they say — still courting to a tremendous party to celebrate the exploit. I expect you were there — most people one knew seemed to be — in a villa in Zamalek. You remember Zamalek? the hoopoes on the lawn which a couple of poor Gyppos were constantly shaving with something that looked like a murderous razor-edged putter, the smell of the warm wet earth, the *flamboyants*, the cannas, the Sudanese servants. It makes me feel positively nostalgic to think of it all. A long way from Tipperary, of course, and even further from the weapon-pits up forward in the desert. But not a bad place to plot *Boy's Own Paper* adventures in. But what about the people who couldn't get out, who had to stay behind and be shot or driven into the mountains or have their villages flattened? At least in Yugoslavia we were fighting real battles, not playing at cowboys and Indians. Do I digress yes, I believe I do. But bear with me because I am getting round to the main point of this monologue, which I shall pack nicely in its box when I have finished and secure it with camera-tape, because it is for your ears only, dear boy, and not to be played back even to Sue and not repeat not to be lent, sold or otherwise made available to your pal, Gilchrist. Then dear widowed Eva will post it on Monday because if I keep it any longer I may be tempted to change my mind and wipe it. What it amounts to, you see, is a full confession. I am, as the saying goes, about to make a clean breast of things. Not just because I want to put the record straight but to put you, my friend, to the test. Because if what is on this tape is leaked there will be only one source and that is you. But first, if you will excuse me, I really must have a leak.

Right. About Greenspan. There is a wonderful story going the rounds of Television Centre that when he was over for that programme — first-class airfare, first-class hotel — he tried to smuggle a young woman up into his bedroom but was spotted by the porter. So they left together — it was quite late — and ended up in an all-night café near King's Cross because he didn't know where to take her and she, poor thing, being apparently a novice at the game, didn't know where to take

him and wanted to get back to Mum in Watford or somewhere. Actually — come to think of it — it's not very funny.
A bit sad, really. But to get back to the matter in hand —
where to begin? Maybe with that trip to Berlin with Ashburton
— who is now, incidentally, involved with some dubiously
funded magazine — when I got so cross, you remember,
about rumours — well, more than rumours, stories, allegations
— that the Russians, the troops who had come all the way
from Stalingrad, were behaving like the proverbial drunk and
licentious soldiery. Well, by the time I was demobbed I had
had to accept that whatever the exaggerations, there was a
solid core of truth to it all. Not easy to accept. Not easy at all.
Nor the way Uncle Joe behaved towards the Yugoslavs, for
that matter — seeking to reduce them to a client state and
threatening invasion if they did not accept his terms. Nor
what was going on inside Yugoslavia either. Men I had known
up there in the mountains above Zelena Gora, good, brave
men, being removed, vilified, gaoled. Then there were all
those grotesque trials — the Slansky trial for instance — and
all the old International Brigaders in the East just disappear-
ing. Liquidated, framed, judicially murdered. The way the
Hungarian rising was put down — although, mind you, I
think the picture was a bit more complicated than the propa-
gandists in the West let on. As a result I went through a kind of
withdrawal process from politics as I understood the word. It
was painful to a degree and might have been irreversible
except that the heart — which as we all know has its own
complicated reasons — disposes me to make allowances, to
come down on one side rather than the other, to go along
sentimentally with people who still have faith and believe in
millenia. But I mustn't ramble. You remember no doubt,
because you've been keeping tabs on me, I'm sure, that after
the war I went to the Courtauld and did a thing on Austrian
Gothic. It was a bit like making a documentary. For a couple
of years I was an expert on the respective merits of the Master
of the Krainburger Altar and the Master of the Linz Crucifixion
and could bandy names and dates about with the best of them.

174

Now it's all incredibly hazy. In any case what really interested me was what you could pick up from the iconography about the material culture of the late Middle Ages in Austria. Which was — how did you guess? — the title of my thesis: *The Material Culture of the late Middle Ages as illustrated by the iconography of the altarpieces and wall-paintings of Lower and Upper Austria*. About living conditions, clothing, furniture, hair styles, architecture, social and personal habits. There's an extraordinary altar-piece in the Tyrol that shows the Virgin sitting up in bed topless, as they say nowadays. But that's clearly not what I want to talk about. In any case, if you're interested there is certainly a copy in the library at the Institute. The candidate will submit two copies of the thesis in hard covers etc. And your friend Gilchrist has seen it — I said he had done his homework, didn't I? Well when I was beavering away at Austrian Gothic and using, I suppose, a sort of residual Marxism or historical materialism — maybe that's more accurate — because it's a matrix which once imprinted on the mind is damnably hard to obliterate, even if one wants to, which I wasn't particularly keen to do anyway — I was asked by someone — a man I had known at Oxford before he went off to drive an ambulance in Spain, although he was much older than me — to do him a favour. I'm going for security reasons to call him N. because I have no intention of telling you who he was or is although Gilchrist does claim to know, the bastard. Well one evening I had dinner at his place — a flat just off Piccadilly — marvellously tasteful, nothing overdone, where he lived with his Spanish boyfriend who had a job in some high-class restaurant and was a wonderful cook. It was a very pleasant evening — good food, good wine — and he had a mass of relics — that's the best word for them — of the Spanish Civil War. Photographs: one of himself and a couple of boyfriends in riding-breeches and big boots in front of an ambulance in Barcelona. An anarchist militiaman's cap which his boyfriend put on and ponced about in which didn't please N. one bit. Posters like the ones I used to own myself but they got lost in the war. Do you remember

175

the posters I used to have in that flat of mine above the Water of Leith, when you were on the fringe of the Party for reasons that are becoming clearer to me, and losing your virginity to poor old Felicity who thought you were terribly innocent and rather sweet? I was off to Austria a couple of days later so N. asked me if I'd do him a favour in Vienna. All I had to do was go to a secondhand bookshop just off the Franziskanerplatz and ask for a copy of a book by Max Dvorak called *Kunstgeschichte als Geistesgeschichte*. It was slightly odd because surely he could have got a copy somewhere in London or Oxford and anyway there was a copy in the Institute library — in fact I had used it because it had a rather good chapter on Gothic painting. But the book was admittedly hard to come by and who was I to ask questions anyway? You may remember from our tape-recording session that I tend not to ask questions. So one morning I trotted off from my hotel — incidentally you must go there if you are ever in Vienna, an extraordinary place just off the Graben, terribly cheap and fairly quiet — and you don't actually have to pick up any of the ladies who are available in the bar in the evening where they sit, chatting and examining their nylons, under an oil-painting — God knows where it came from, an auction, I suppose — of a very upper-class lady in a decolleté evening dress who looks down disapprovingly on the line-up of talent on the bar-stools. Which is all an immense diversion on my part, dear John, because I am feeling my way towards a point of pain in my memory, probing forward the way one's tongue probes towards a little ulcer in the soft wet flesh of cheek or gum. So to resume: one morning I trotted off from my hotel, which at that time of day was utterly respectable with what looked like a honeymoon couple from the provinces taking breakfast in the bar — I trotted off, I say, and found the place without too much trouble. It was an extraordinary shop. Full of stuff that had somehow survived the Nazi times. A first edition of Freud's *Interpretation of Dreams*. That book by Weininger — I can't think of the title — about Jewish self-hate. That sort of thing. The owner was very civil; middle-aged, respectable-looking,

176

knowledgeable too. He asked kindly after N. — I assumed he was another member of the club — and went off into the backshop to collect the volume so I got chatting to his assistant. She was rather small, dark-haired, with brown eyes and a face — how shall I describe it to you? — pointed, quizzical, animated. Perhaps she was Magyar by descent. Although I had seen women like her in mountain villages in the Tyrol. After the owner had come back with the book nicely parcelled up I stayed on chatting with her. Before I left we had arranged to meet that evening and go out by tram to Grinzing to drink the new season's wine, eat goose-dripping sandwiches — have you ever tried *Gänseschmalz?* Full of cholesterol no doubt, but delicious — and listen to *Schrammelmusik.* Well, one thing, as they say, led to another and for the next three weeks as I travelled round looking at churches I used her flat as a base. Very old it was and looked out on to a courtyard with geraniums on the balconies. Right under the roof so that you had to watch not to bang your head on the sloping ceiling. A room with almost no furniture: cushions on the floor, a mattress, posters on the walls. At home she wore a kind of kimono that made her look very eastern, almost Turkish. Over the roof-tops you could see the roof of the Stefansdom, like some huge aerofoil banking in the sky. Do I bore you? I expect I do. So I won't go on about the things we saw together, from the Klimts in the Belvedere to the Adolf Loos House in the Michaelerplatz, that plain building which — long ago, before the First World War — confronted Franz Josef in his Imperial palace and sent the right-wing — including no doubt an amateur of architecture called Adolf Hitler, who was in Vienna and down on his luck — into paroxysms of rage. Whoever said aesthetics have no bearing on politics? If you're interested why don't you take a look at Vienna, City of Dreams, produced and directed by Colin Elphinstone, which goes out — unless I'm greatly mistaken — sometime this coming week and which I very much hope I shall make it back for, if I'm spared. Do you remember from our Scottish youth how the old ladies used to say that? Anyway look out for what

177

I think is a stunning shot that ends up on that very house — a travelling one coming into the Michaelerplatz, past the Redoutensaal — the way she and I walked together, laughing at the figures on the front of the Hofburg writhing in the last convulsions of the classical style — which as you no doubt have guessed is a quote from the commentary. She could be immensely funny with a kind of anarchic humour that reminded me — did I mention that she knew him? — of that old acquaintance of yours, a producer in the BBC German Service, with a brown tonsure and a nicely cynical attitude towards his work. Herlitschka! That's the name. Who was — as I recall — some sort of Hampstead radical. She herself was very hard to place. What she did during the war I have no idea. People had to live — had to get by — and she got by. Except that one day from the tram she pointed to what was obviously a prison and said: They beheaded a working-class girl of eighteen there in 1944 for distributing leaflets. And the judge who sentenced her lives on a state pension. If I say she was great fun that's true but inadequate. She was a joyful person, witty and deeply serious at the same time. I cannot remember feeling so much at ease, so much myself, so little on my guard as in her company, in her flat, in her arms. When I had to go she helped me pack. Handed over N.'s book and told me to take care of it. I put it carefully in the bottom of my case. I said I wanted to see her again. She laughed and said she had learned not to count on things, not to plan too far ahead, that in her experience 'das Beste im Leben ist umsonst'. How would you translate that, with your degree in German? I suppose it means that the best things in life are — as it were — gratis. A gift from the gods, you might say.

I got back and gave N. his book for which he was duly grateful. Not long afterwards he found himself a grander job and handed me over to a good lady, very Bloomsbury, who found my thesis pretty boring but put up with me because she was a great snob and I impressed her by dropping a couple of names — friends of my mother's from the days when she used to do the London season, the summer

178

exhibition at the Academy, that sort of thing — and had some sort of entrée into the Bloomsbury set. I wrote to Zdenka — did I say her name was Zdenka? — once or twice but got no reply. Which didn't bother me because I didn't expect her to be a great letter-writer. Then just over a year later I was in Vienna again and went to the shop. It had changed hands. No, they had no idea where the previous owner had gone. So I went round to the flat. The name was different but I rang just the same. A young man came to the door. When I asked for Zdenka he gave me a funny look and asked if I were a friend of hers. I said I was. In that case he was sorry. Didn't I know? She had committed suicide some months ago. No, I said, I didn't know and went back and got drunk in my hotel off the Graben.

Now, my dear and very secure friend, and master of such mysteries, will you read me a riddle? This is how it goes.

N. asks me to go to a secondhand bookshop in Vienna and pick up a book. Which is perfectly natural and comprehensible because the book in question is rare and quite hard to find except in rather specialized bookshops. I go to Vienna, find the shop and the bookseller gives me the book. Meantime I fall in love — whatever that may mean — with his assistant. I come back to England and give N. his book. He leaves the Courtauld. A year later the bookshop has changed hands. The owner has vanished — retired to Ischia, perhaps, where the Italian boys lie on the rocks like seals and wait for custom — and the assistant has committed suicide for any one of those reasons that make human beings end their own lives. A head-long fall into a pit of despair, *chagrins d'amour*, some sort of exhaustion, loneliness, *tedium vitae*. You can take your pick since to be honest I did not know her well enough to hazard a plausible guess. As you can see it is a banal story devoid of causality. A series of events in time requiring no elucidation.

So far so good and so clear, but now the riddle begins. Let's see what it looks like if we let a quantum of paranoia enter our minds — paranoia which finds causalities everywhere and locks us into conspiracies, knowing, as you do and I do, that a trace of paranoid suspicion is probably essential for all good intelligence work although it has to be used with caution. Because it can lead to a sequence of take and double-take, bluff and double-bluff, in which the simple truth is lost. Let me just change the tape and I will demonstrate how it works.

Right. I am back. I have turned the tape. I have tested it not by counting up to four or telling it who I am — which I believe I still know although doubts do creep in — and what I had for breakfast but by confiding to it some banalities — thoughts about love and pain — which are no business of yours and which I have therefore wiped. So let me restate things with, as I say, that dash of paranoia. Then the story goes like this. N. asks me to pick up a book in Vienna because he knows I once was hooked on a millenium and still cling — against all the evidence — to a vestigial hope that, perhaps, out of the blood and suffering and shit and in spite of the lies, the killings, the mockeries of justice committed in the name of Communism, a seed of hope will some day spring somewhere on this benighted planet, maybe even in the East, and that we shall see not the millenium, but a prospect of a new and better society. So he reckons that I will not ask questions about my errand — my mission if you like — whatever you care to call it, although I may have my niggling suspicions and find it fishy — to say the least — that he can't get this particular book through one of the bookshops in London or Oxford where he is a known and respected customer. Anyway Joe Soak picks the book up from a gentleman who has interests beyond the antiquarian book-trade and Zdenka, who with all her droll charm was always *undurchsichtig* — unseethroughable — is for her own reasons solicitous in seeing that I don't lose it or forget it, but take it safely home with me. If so is her friendship — to borrow a phrase — mere feigning and our loving mere folly? But maybe that is a question you are not competent to answer. A year later her boss has disappeared, because things have got too hot for him, and Zdenka is dead. For reasons that escape still me perhaps because I refuse to contemplate them. So what do you make of that, you who can smell out rats so precisely? But I have not finished.

Enter now your friend Gilchrist, with his fox's face, a prince of darkness and of paranoias to whom you are — I take it — some sort of *famulus*, an apprentice sorcerer, a very minor devil, and in whose ear — for who could it be but you? — you have sown the suspicion that I betrayed that famous tunnel under the Wall. Enter, I say, Gilchrist with his foot in the door — after inumerable telephone calls — so that for the sake of peace and quiet and just to get him off my back I ask him in. He is very gracious and finds the flat to his liking. Praises the malt whisky I offer him. Claims some sort of mystical kinship in the name of Scotland and auld lang syne and proposes the toast 'Here's tae us wha's like us' and then gets down to business. And does a tale unfold. Which is that he believes that I knowingly went to Vienna to undertake a mission for N., whom he does not hesitate to describe as a traitor, that I went straight to the bookshop where the owner, who has since been 'turned' as they say in your magic circles, handed me a book in which the first 'i' in — here he produced a piece of paper with the title typewritten on it — *Kunstgeschichte* was for his money probably a microdot. Zdenka was a Communist from away back and did her job like any good Communist under orders and got me into bed to see that the book got back safely. She was — you know how he grins — apparently an attractive young woman with quite a history. No, he couldn't tell me how he knew, or what his sources were for all this. But he had been in the business for a while and I'd be surprised the places he could get in to and the people — high heid yins tae — he could chat to the way we were chatting now. Why did she commit suicide? Maybe she just cracked up. Maybe they wanted her to go back behind the Iron Curtain and she was frightened. Maybe she made a mess of some assignment. I could take my choice. But it wasn't all that interesting. The point was this: he, Gilchrist, had enough stuff to write up an interesting story about an art student with a CP background, not to mention an interesting sex-life, who was wandering

181

about Austria — all that stuff about frescoes was just cover — in contact with a known agent in Vienna, and controlled by you know who. Someone who went on to be a big name in the media, someone who had interesting friends like Tom Pressman — no doubt the name would ring a bell — and interesting connections in the so-called German Democratic Republic. Who, there were good reasons for thinking, betrayed to the East Germans the existence of a tunnel under the Berlin Wall and had thereby been responsible for the deaths and imprisonment of brave men and women. It would be a great Sunday morning's read but wouldn't, he imagined, do my career any good. He couldn't see the Beeb wanting to use me much. Nor anybody else for that matter. And forget about visas to the States. However there were other bigger fish in the sea than me and maybe I could help to catch them. If for instance I was prepared to give him an exclusive on N., who was in any case one of those upper-class queers who has been getting away with murder for far too long just because he went to the right school and the right university and has a cousin on the Tory front bench, I would no doubt do myself a power of good with certain quarters — he happened to know they were rather interested in me — and incidentally give him the story of the year and of his lifetime. In return he would spike that other story about the art student. Because after all fair is fair. So what did I think? I said I thought he ought to get out. Quick.

Do you understand what I mean when I say that Gilchrist's version has about it the plausibility of a dream from which I do not know how to escape, for I have the feeling of being caught — as the saying goes — between the devil and the deep blue sea. But perhaps old Zeus will stoop out of the sky and bear me up into safety, deposit me on Mount Ida beside the black and comforting dugs of the goat-nymph. And so I maunder on as the raki loosens my tongue and the tape rolls and unrolls until I press the button to stop it. Now!

The announcer paused at the end of a story about the transfer of a player from one football club to another for some astonishing sum and assumed a solemn expression. It was learned today, she said after a caesura, a beat, the intake of a breath, that Colin Elphinstone (a photograph filled the screen) well-known to viewers as the presenter of *Facets*, the much acclaimed programme on the arts, has been accidentally killed while filming in Crete. Colin Elphinstone enjoyed, the voice went on while Colin looked out at me with a slight smile, his hair falling softly over his brow so that I almost expected him to put up a hand with a familiar gesture to brush it away, an international reputation as a television performer and film-maker. *The Beehive Tombs*, his documentary on Etruscan art, won first prize in the documentary class at the Italia Prize this year. His last film, *Vienna, City of Dreams*, will be transmitted later this week. Pause. And now the weather —

The set was high on the wall above the bar. At the other end Grace and Malcolm were bickering unheedingly over the exact placing of a postcard from Madagascar. I sat for a few minutes then got up, found my coat and walked towards the door without a Goodnight. 'Cat got his tongue then,' said Grace. I felt her eyes on me till the door swung to behind me.

I took the tube to Belsize Park and walked towards Sue's flat past the pub where poor Ruth Ellis shot her lover and so intertwined sex and death that on the morning of her execution the British public lay in bed in a guilty state of collective orgasm. There was no light in her ground-floor windows. Behind the front-door Penelope whimpered at my approach. A few years before I would have had a key, let myself in and rescued the bitch for a run on the Heath; but key rights had long been withdrawn with other rights. To pass the time I wandered over the railway bridge that leads to the Heath and watched the obscure traffic below: commuter trains, a diesel

183

locomotive on its own, goods trains oddly strung together. Simply to attend to such irrelevant extraneous phenomena was a numbing agent, a barrier to my guilts. I walked up the dark hill and through the trees on to the bare summit where, in earlier, better days, I had walked with Sue on Sunday afternoons to watch the kite-flyers. The feel of the wind on the crest reminded me of the dunes at home and the tug of the string as our home-made kites, put together from brown paper and bamboo canes, rose landwards on the east wind. 'You should get yourself a kite,' she used to say and I would agree but the months passed and then the time passed when she was interested whether I had a kite or not. The wing-light of a plane hung above London like a green star as I turned downhill over the long damp grass. Unless she had gone to a pub she must be back soon; if she had gone to a pub I might as well go home. As I approached her gate I heard the putter of a moped behind me. Penelope heard it too and began to whine excitedly. Sue pulled her bike into the garden path and pad-locked it to the railing without a word. She was booted; her crash helmet was medieval; when she removed it her hair was cut short — her Joan of Arc look, I called it. Opening the door she bent down to pull Penelope's ears. She spoke gently to the beast then turning to me said: 'I wasn't expecting you but now you're here you can take her for a run. I've got a headache so I'll lie down for a minute.' I knew that if her migraine was on her there was no point in talking yet. When we returned Penelope was wet-pawed and muddy. Sue was in a house-coat with a whisky on the table beside which she reclined. 'Oh God,' she said, 'couldn't you have kept her out of the mud at least.' I did not reply but poured myself a drink. I needed one badly. She watched sharply as I poured.

'Did you see the six o'clock news?'

'Of course not. Why?'

'Colin's dead. Killed filming in Crete.'

'Well,' said Sue, 'that's that. The Snark has escaped you.'

'Is that all you have to say?'

'What the hell do you expect me to say? I tell you what —

maybe we should send a joint wreath. Love from Sue and John for auld lang syne. Something like that.'

'No,' I said and left her to her misery and the rest of the bottle of whisky.

The memorial service was in St Mary-Le-Strand, which lies caught like a boulder in the stream of the traffic under the stone bluffs of Bush House. The congregation was what one might have expected. There were BBC executives in sober suits, programme people too, puzzling over the order of service and not too familiar with the hymns, including someone I identified as Eva, who was overcome and wept a little at the point when Colin was named. Just outside the door someone from *The Times* took the names of the mourners. Not all of us would rate a mention. I have no idea who arranged the service nor who invited us. But they had not missed any of the main characters, so to speak. Diana was there, still looking blonde and upper class. Sue came in late and stood glumly at the back near the door. The service was conducted by a clergyman friend of Colin's who from being a cheerful atheist painter and chaser of skirts had been converted to a leftish kind of Anglicanism. The lesson, read by the actor who did the commentaries on all Colin's documentaries, was that great text of St Paul's: Though I speak with the tongue of men and of angels, which made me think of Colin on the box charming with the flicker of a smile thoughts out of artists and dancers and writers — including poor old Semyonov — thoughts which left them, one could see it from their faces, somewhat surprised even as they uttered them. Then the preacher spoke of Colin, the pilgrim. A poet whose work Colin loved had said that the mind has mountains, cliffs of fall, even more dangerous than those on which he lost his life in Crete and the non-believer needs immense courage to negotiate them. Only those who knew him well would know what it had cost our brother, Colin, to climb among these high and terrible peaks. They would carry the memory of him in their hearts as of one who had been lovely and pleasant in his life — a man who had shown the same generosity of spirit and the same courage in all aspects of it — as a soldier, as a communicator, in his political beliefs. After that the hymn could only be Bunyan's *To be a pilgrim* with its tramping four-square tune. As we discreetly jostled our way out I was able to say a brief Hello to Diana, who did not, I think, remember who I was. Sue had fled the moment the service was over and the organ began to play, swept down the steps by the cascades of a Bach toccata. By the gate there was Gilchrist himself. He grinned when I saw him. Was he covering the event, I asked, or was he there the way the plain clothes boys attend the funeral after a murder. He wasn't sure how to take it but said what had brought him was professional curiosity. He suggested a drink but, for once, I didn't feel like one. He went on for a bit about the priest who had conducted the service and how he was one of a whole gang of Reds who had managed to get into the C of E, where they preached pacifism and anti-nuclear cant. He was going to do a big piece on them one of these days. Then, as he put it, he felt he must toddle off towards Fleet Street to file a story but stopped, retraced his steps and said: 'What do you think — did he jump or was he pushed?' 'Pushed,' I replied. 'By you and me.' Gilchrist laughed uncertainly. For a moment he thought then said: 'You know, Jock, there's a real story there. Someone should write it and I don't have time. Any way it's water under the bridge. History, you might say.'

MORE CARCANET FICTION

For a catalogue describing these and other books on the Carcanet list, write to: Carcanet Press, 208–212 Corn Exchange Buildings, Manchester M4 3BQ, or: Carcanet, 198 Sixth Avenue, New York, New York 10013.

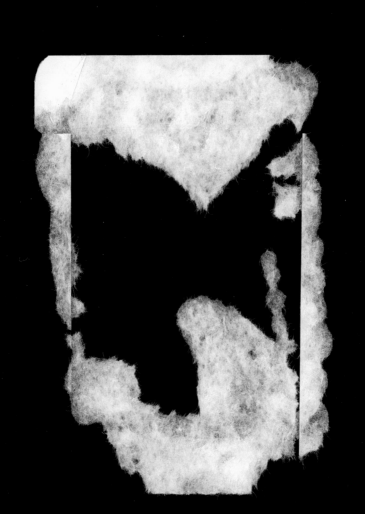